The Forever 39ers

by

Shari Busa Ortiz

To my son, Chris, who unwittingly gave me the gift of free time by going away to college for 4 years. To my husband, Rich, who drove me crazy with his need to find the most acceptable name for his character, despite the fact that the book is really about women! Then again, I spent many a night writing at Starbucks, so he gets a pass on the name issue. Both of my guys provided me with lots of fodder for the story, so for that they get a very special and loving thank you.

To my dear friend, Donna Baez Chaffin, who was my inspiration for the character, Kate. We have been laughing together since grammar school, and even at the ripe-old-age of "39," we still manage to maintain our silly and immature personalities.

And lastly to my other dear friend, Sue Fischer: this book never would have come to fruition without you as not only my grueling editor, but as my biggest champion, supporter and BELIEVER! Thank you for continuing to push even when I grew obstinate and pushed back.

For Max, my "Oliver," who put a smile on my face and love in my heart every day of his life. May your happy spirit live on through my story.

Table of Contents:

CHAPTER 1—TURNING FIFTY

"Yikes!"

"Holy crap!"

I turned from the sink as my husband, Vic, ran into the kitchen, followed by one of my best friends. Kate yelled, "He walked in on me while I was in my bra and panties!" The look on her face was priceless.

"How was I supposed to know that you were undressed?" replied Vic. "It's not as

if the door was locked!"

"Well, this is my room while I'm staying here, and I would like to think I can expect some privacy when the door is *closed*!" Kate yelled again as she performed a barefoot pivot and stomped off.

She must have picked up a nightshirt to cover herself

before she came into the kitchen. I had no idea whether she realized that her scantily clad rear end was wiggling and jiggling as she left the room in a huff. *So much for modesty,* I thought. I covered my mouth and turned back to the sink to keep from laughing aloud. In the process, I caught a glimpse of my husband's face, which mirrored Kate's appalled expression. He, too, walked away muttering something about being "scarred for life."

My friend was in my house getting dressed because today was my fiftieth birthday and tonight was the big, celebratory shindig at our local VFW hall. I would have liked to celebrate the main event at a more upscale establishment. I was thinking along the lines of a well-known New Jersey banquet hall made popular by an also very well-known television series. My somewhat thrifty husband had been geared up for a backyard party replete with latex balloons, party store paper tablecloths, and homemade banners. The VFW hall was the compromise setting. As far as I knew, the paper tablecloths had been upgraded to plastic, the balloons were made of Mylar, and the banners were still homemade.

It was good, I decided. There would be plenty of food, drink, and DJ music and a room full of family and friends. What more could a girl ask for?

June 24, 2010 was my fiftieth birthday. I'd been married twenty-four years to a great guy, Vic Castillo, and we had one seventeen-year-old son, Neil. Completing the family were a cairn terrier, Oliver, and a guinea pig, Pig.

We decided to call him Pig because three intelligent people could not come up with a name for this small creature. Calling him Guinea would not have been the most politically correct choice and could have caused all manner of negative feedback. We might have even seen a rock or two come flying through our window.

Oh, and I almost forgot our two geckos, Millie and Speedy. There wasn't much to say about them other than that they were sweet, didn't make noise, and didn't cause any trouble. Unlike Oliver. My only problem with them was that they ate live crickets. The eating of live animals and insects was definitely not on my top-ten list of things to watch, so I refrained from this particular form of animal care and left it up to Vic and Neil. Anything else animal-related, I was your go-to woman. Just no live-feeding for me!

There was a cute little story surrounding the addition of Millie and Speedy to our family. When Neil was seven years old, he decided to ask Santa Claus for a puppy for Christmas. At that time, we already had a black Labrador retriever named Max, who, although entering his senior years, was definitely not going any time soon to wherever dogs go after they've passed on. A second dog was out of the question as far as Vic was concerned, and yet I had the sweetest "Dear Santa" letter tucked away in my top desk drawer.

A few weeks before that Christmas, I was telling a friend about my dilemma and she responded with, "How would you like a couple of four-year-old geckos that I'm looking to get rid of? My boys want hamsters for Christmas, but there's just no way that I'm taking care of hamsters AND geckos!" I swore that at that moment, a huge, flashing neon sign appeared before my eyes saying, "Problem solved!" To this day, I still think it was a "sign" from God. Whatever the case, Millie and Speedy came to be part of the Castillo family.

I considered Kate to be part of our family, too. She is one of my best friends, and I've known her for thirty-eight years. She's married and worked in Manhattan as an interior designer. She decided that my birthday weekend should also be a girls' weekend, so she was staying at my house, where we could do lots of girl talk, wine drinking, and then slurred, silly girl talk followed by passing out in bed. That was what last night amounted to, at any rate, and I had no doubt that after my party, tonight would be a repeat performance. I loved Kate. She made me laugh all the time, especially when I was feeling down and out. When she walked into a room, it was as if a sun-filled gust of wind had entered. When she left, the room felt empty.

The doorbell rang, and before I had taken two steps, in walked my mother-in-law, Maria, who yelled something that contained the words, "¿Qué pasó?" and "gritos." Now, I knew that "¿Qué pasó?" meant "What happened?" but I was lost on "gritos." My mother-in-law lived right next door to us. I mean *right* next door, and because of that, two things frequently happened. The first was that she knew *all* of our comings and goings. That didn't bother me as much as the second thing, which was that she felt she had the right to let herself into our house at any time. It was always the same: she'd ring the doorbell while inserting the door key and letting herself in. After many "running-naked-to-hastily-dress" experiences, we'd all gotten into the habit of always having clothes on. We just never knew when Mama Castillo would come

waltzing through the door. At one point, I started showering with a bathing suit on, but that became a little awk-
ward when washing certain areas, so I had to give it up.
Let's just say that nowadays the bathroom door was never unlocked when occupied.

Mama, as we called her, did not speak much English.
She was born and raised in Spain and never worked outside the home after she came to the United States. Also,
Vic and his brother, Pete, always spoke to their mother in
Spanish, so she was never given much opportunity to
learn English. Sometimes I thought she knew more than
she let on, but she always spoke Spanish to me, so we had
a bit of a communication barrier. I think she did it on
purpose, too, just to frustrate me. When I was in high
school and college, I took the basic Spanish courses, so
while Vic and I were dating and through our first years of
marriage, I could have some semblance of a conversation
with her. Well, I've long since lost my Spanish-speaking
skills, so most of the time I nodded and smiled if her face
looked happy, and I frowned and *tsk-tsk* when she looked
unhappy or mad. Don't get me wrong: this was not the
best way to handle the situation. I'd more than once given
inappropriate responses, which landed me on Mama's
shit list. Trust me, that wasn't a place you really wanted
to be!

My father-in-law, Pedro, was an easy-to-get-along-
with guy. Unlike his wife, he spoke English, but, also unlike his wife, he couldn't hear and refused to wear his
hearing aid. All of our conversations were punctuated by
the question "What?" After several attempts at getting my
point across, I simply gave up. On the other hand, the

man was happy to stay in his own home, minding his own business, sitting in his own chair, and reading his own newspaper, so who was I to complain? If he could just keep his wife at home with him, life would be good.

I looked at the clock. It was time to get ready for the big party. "Getting ready" seemed to have become a much lengthier process than it was when I was younger. I thought that two hours should be enough time. I shaved, showered, and was in the middle of putting on my anti-wrinkle, firming, take-ten-years-off facial moisturizer when in walked Kate. For a moment I wondered if Mama Castillo had sent her, but then I shook my head. I sometimes forgot, since I didn't live with her, that Kate was also prone to barging in unannounced.

She looked me up and down and commented, "Boy, your boobs look big! Is that a push-up bra? Where did you get it? Can I feel it?" Then she reached out and attempted to grab me. Fortunately, at the same time I took a step back and avoided being woman-handled. Kate had never been one to mince words. When I was seven months pregnant with Neil, she and I went to the beach one hot July day. She took one look at me in my one-piece maternity bathing suit and declared that I had "tree-trunk legs," which is just what every half-naked, self-conscious, seven-months-pregnant woman wants to hear.

I kicked Kate out and studied myself in the mirror. *I really don't look that bad for fifty,* I thought. My face was relatively smooth, with some crow's feet around the eyes and laugh lines around the mouth. I've always been a big smiler, so I assumed that was to be expected. I detected a slight facial droop, so I pulled my face up at the temples.

Hmm. Much better! I had green eyes and long, straight, medium-brown hair, and I thought I was considered somewhat attractive. At least, that's what people told me. I was by no means beautiful, so I was happy with being called "attractive." I was five feet three inches tall and 115 pounds on a "skinny" day. From my teens until I turned forty, I was a very content 103 pounds. Apparently, for women, the arrival of their forties brings with it all manner of mental and physical changes. One of my biggest and most depressing changes was my ability to gain weight simply by looking at food. I'm not kidding! A swift glance at the window-displayed cakes in my local bakery was an instant one-to-two pound gain. I had spent my forties averting my gaze from all food that I had no intention of eating. If I wasn't going to eat it, then I certainly wasn't going to allow myself to gain weight just by looking at it. Despite my best efforts, by the age of forty-eight, I was 130 pounds and climbing, so I put my up-a-half-size foot down, hit the local Weight Watchers, and started a rigorous exercise regimen. I might never see 103 pounds on the scale again, but that was fine by me. My current weight seemed to agree with me, and eating carrots and celery sticks as healthy late-night snacks had gotten old.

I should be honest about my "straight" hair. It was really a mix of curly, wavy, frizzy hair depending on the level of humidity. I tried to keep this fact a secret. It had been this way since I was a kid, and I *hated* it! For many years, I permed my hair after Barbara Streisand in "A Star Is Born." She popularized perms for many women. For me, they gave my hair a less frizzy, more attractive curl. I was always jealous of the girls with the long, straight, swingy hair in the L'Oréal commercials, so as I got older, I started doing everything possible to straighten my hair. The invention of flatirons was a blessing for me. With the exception of vacations and the anonymity that went along with them, I always kept my hair straight, much to the dismay of my friends and family, who claimed they loved my wild, curly look.

"Hey, Mom! Dad and I have to shower too," yelled Neil while banging on the door. I guessed inspection time was over, and I opened the door to my son's exasperated impatient face. "Did you leave me any hot water?" he asked as I walked by. I kept my mouth shut as I thought of the countless forty-five minute showers he'd taken, but Neil was a teenage boy and I'd been told that this was quite normal behavior. Apparently, teenage boys liked to study every new hair that grew and every muscle that developed. They did this at various angles until they found the angle that enhanced their bodily appearance the best.

I remembered when I was a blossoming, pre-teen/teenager and would check every day to see if there was any new breast growth. Sadly, by thirteen, I had hit my maximum bra size of 34B and, with the exception of during pregnancy, was never to see anything bigger. To this day, I still envied those women with C's and above, and I thought that men did too, or rather they found them more appealing than the less endowed ones. They'd tell you that a "handful" is good enough, but I really thought they lied just to make us small-chested women feel better. And let's face it: those lying men were usually our husbands!

I've been married twenty-four years, and when people exclaim, "Doesn't it only seem like yesterday that you got married?" I look at them like they have four heads. "No," I answer. "It seems like I've been married twenty-four years."

Although, as I glanced back at my bathroom-bound seventeen-year-old, I thought that those years had flown by. Gone were the days when Mom was the next best thing to peanut butter (which was coincidentally Neil's daily lunch for six grammar school years). Up until high school, he couldn't wait to rush home from school to tell me all about his day, his teachers, and his friends. With the arrival of freshman year came the loss of my son's communicative skills. The only words he seemed adept at now were "Uh-huh," "I don't know," and "I don't remember," punctuated by grunts. I thought this meant that he was approaching manhood, but that was just a guess on my part and solely based on my husband's behavior.

Speaking of my husband and son and seventeen years ago, I thought of the day that Neil was born and how he got his name. I had picked out two names, Kate for a girl and Neil for a boy. Obviously, Kate would be named after my best friend, plus I really did love the name. Neil was to be named after my favorite singer/songwriter/musician, Neil Young. Vic fought me tooth and nail on that one, and we had finally settled on Joseph as a name, somewhat to my dismay. I'll never admit this to Vic, but I used my labor to my advantage. As I screamed, sweated, writhed, and grunted through the birth of our son, I somehow found the mental acuity to force my husband to promise that after all of this "suffering," I would be able to pick the name of *my* choice. So, as I screamed in pain, I also shouted out, "*If this baby is a boy, I want him to be called Neil! I deserve this small concession from you!*"

Vic never knew what hit him. As he cried my tears, felt my pain, and took every Lamaze breath with me, he yelled back, "*Whatever you want, honey! Whatever you want!*" and Neil was born. I learned a very valuable lesson that day. Drama, pain, and tears can go very far with your spouse. You just have to know when and where to play your cards.

At that moment, Vic walked into the bedroom and gave me a strange, sideways look, as I was laughing to myself while alone. He was used to it and claimed that I also was prone to laughing in my sleep, but it still struck him as a bit strange. He and I possessed totally different senses of humor, which meant that I laughed at everything and he didn't. Vic tended to be more of a quiet, serious guy, which I supposed was why he did so well in his position as Chief Financial Officer of a hospital. Despite our differences in humor, we were very compatible. Our only problems and arguments stemmed from Vic's thinking that he was also a CFO in our household. Besides wanting to control each expenditure that we made, he also leaned towards the frugal side. I was more of a "You can't take it with you when you go" kind of girl, which usually led to a monthly brawl between us when the credit card bills arrived. He was also a "Worry about the future" guy, whereas I was a "Take it day by day" woman. Well, it *is* said that opposites attract. Although I don't really believe that we're opposites, I think we balance each other out nicely.

I tried not to pay attention as he pulled out three dress shirts. "Which one goes good with the black pants?" he asked as he always did.

They're black pants. They all go, I thought, but didn't say it out loud. I knew he was really looking for me to make his attire decision for him as I usually did, so I said, "I like the brown- and black-striped shirt. You'll look very good in it." For as long as we've been married, I have purchased my husband's clothes, from underwear and socks to suits and coats. I thought if it were up to him, he'd still be wearing the clothes from the early 1980s when we met. It was true and it scared me, so I made sure that at Christmas and birthdays there was an abundance of clothing gifts for him. For whatever reason, these gifts were OK by him, and he wouldn't turn them down. He just wouldn't go out and buy the apparel on his own. I also thought that this might have to do with his absolute hatred of shopping and the fact that he had to part with money when doing so.

An hour later, everyone was dressed and ready to go, so we piled into two cars and got ready to head the mile or so to the VFW hall. Neil was in charge of driving my in-laws to the party because we all couldn't fit into one car. I felt a little sorry for him since getting my father-in-law out of the house could be a challenge. Papa Castillo was neurotic, so leaving the house, even for just a short period of time, involved checking and rechecking the oven to make sure that it was off, unplugging all appliances, locking the front door, and then going back numerous times to make sure that it was indeed locked. All of this was followed by a brief walk around the outside of the house to ensure that no windows had been left ajar. I always wondered if his obsessive-compulsive behavior was why he tended to stay home frequently, as leaving seemed to be exhausting, time-consuming work. I saw Vic smirk as I happily waved good-bye to Neil, and thought, *Better him than me!*

CHAPTER 2—MEET THE FAMILY

The six of us were the first to arrive, but we wanted to get there early just to make sure that all was in order. Vic and Neil had gone earlier to set up, and I thought they'd done a great job. Everything was decorated in turquoise and black. The centerpieces had turquoise flowers with white baby's breath, accentuated by transparent turquoise and black Mylar balloons in the middle of the flowers. My original plan was to wear a coordinating dress, but a hot black-and-white zebra number caught my eye about a year before the party, and I bought it. My friends swore up, down, and sideways that I would be sick of the dress before I ever wore it. I actually thought they had bets going that I would break down at the last minute and buy another dress. Well, the joke was on them. Not only had I

hung the dress in the back of my walk-in closet and forgotten about it, but I also purchased shoes that were an
exact match. Some women want to be cougars. Apparently, I wished to be a zebra.

"Well, what a pain in the neck finding *this* place! I
was ready to tell her father to turn around and go right
back home. I'm sure everyone will get lost coming." Oh
no! I cringed as I heard my ever-complaining mother's
voice.

"Stop exaggerating, Gloria. It wasn't hard to find at
all," said my dad, as usual bringing my excitable mother
back down to reality. I briefly considered hiding somewhere until more people arrived. I could blend into the
crowd, thus ignoring my mother, but I knew I was being
unrealistic and she would find me.

"Jill. Oh, Jill! There you are! Where should I hang
my jacket?"

Was she serious? It was the end of June! Yes, she
was serious. She had not only a jacket but also the ever-
present, highly-embarrassing-to-her-children kerchief
covering her hair. I reached out to help her remove it before anyone else walked in and saw it.

"Stop that, Jill! You're going to mess my hair. I just
went to the beauty parlor today to have it done for your
party!"

I still cannot get my mother to say "salon." She in-
sists on "beauty parlor." I guess it's an age thing. I sadly
use that expression often to describe my mother. The
woman had a *kerchief* on her head! She claimed it was
multifunctional, as it kept her hair in place and her head
warm. It was June. She literally went from her house to

the car so I didn't understand why she needed it today, but the fact was that a kerchief to my mother was what a teddy bear was to a small child. It was a comfort zone. I didn't know exactly what she thought was going to happen if she gave it up, but apparently she had some deep-seated fears. At least today's headpiece was white to match her jacket. I've seen her in the animal-print one, and it wasn't a pretty sight!

We stood there inspecting each other, which was par for the course for us. Wow! No polyester pants! What was with that? Polyester pants were another of Mom's daily staples that she refused to give up. Her reasoning behind the pants was "They're comfortable. They're wash-and-wear," and—the worst, in my opinion—"They come in so many colors." Sadly, she seemed to have all of those colors too. Tonight she had on a dark skirt and a floral blouse, and I was proud of her. Wait! On closer inspection, I saw that the skirt was polyester! Well, the lights would be dim and hopefully no one would notice. If I was honest with myself, I'd admit that my mom's lack of taste in clothing really only drew the attention of her children, but then again, I wasn't quite sure, so I'd remain embarrassed.

"Honey, don't you think that dress is a little garish? Why didn't you wear the peach dress?"

I gaped at her. "Ma! That dress is twenty years old and hasn't been in style since I wore it to Pete and Gabriella's wedding! Are you kidding me?"

"Who cares how old it is! It looked so pretty on you," she answered.

Just as I opened my mouth to give a sarcastic retort,

my dad walked over, put his arm around me, and said, "You look beautiful as always, Jill. Happy birthday, sweetheart." It was just like my dad to throw water on the mother/daughter fire. It had been this way since I was a kid. My mother and I were very different people and prone to clashing time and again. Dad, on the other hand, was a less critical, more stable presence for his children, so we all tended to gravitate to him when we wanted to talk about something important or were just looking for attention. Unlike my mother, he was *not* wearing polyester, but rather black dress pants with a black dress shirt that I thought made him look very handsome.

What can I say? I have been and always will be "daddy's little girl." *Well, at least one of them,* I thought as my sister and her husband entered the hall, followed closely by my brother with his woman of the week. As usual, I didn't know her.

I probably wouldn't get to know her either; my brother, Anthony, went through women almost as fast as babies go through diapers. As was typical, this one was tall and blond and had big boobs. He'd introduce me to her, and I'd forget her name before he was even done saying it. I'd pretty much taken (not to their faces, of course) to calling them all "Blondie." It didn't really matter what I called them, since most of the time, the first meeting was also the last.

Anthony waved to me and then walked over to Vic, said "Hi!" and introduced his new bimbo. As usual, I watched Vic's eyes bulge out of their sockets as if he were a kid in a candy store. I supposed that big breasts really were a treat for him.

My brother was something of a millionaire wannabe. His occupation was as an exterminator, but his real dream was to invent something big, something that would garner a lot of money and notoriety, thus earning him a spot on the Forbes list.

Since he lived in a true bachelor pad, he tended to use our basement and sometimes our yard to "invent" and to test his "inventions." Let's just say the police and fire department knew us very well. Mama Castillo had taken to putting her house in "lockdown" every time she saw his truck drive up. Actually, that worked for me, too.

Our younger sister, Kelly, was the extreme opposite of Anthony and me. Where we tended to be more outgoing and overall happy people, she was quiet and reserved. Her husband, Jim, was also quiet, as were their two children, who were the most well-behaved children I'd ever met. I thought this was the reason that she and Mom got along the best of the three of us. They didn't fight. If Mom got on Kelly's nerves, Kelly didn't let it show like Anthony and I did. Kelly was the youngest, too, so our mother had always doted on her. Anthony, by virtue of his being a male, had earned "mama's boy" status. Apparently I, the oldest, had been left out in the cold once the boy and then the youngest were born. Sometimes I thought Mama Castillo wished that Kelly had been the one to marry her son.

"Wow! Look how great this place looks! Jill, your dress is perfect! It's so *you*!" exclaimed my Aunt Marie as she came up to me followed by her husband, Uncle Al.

Aunt Marie was my dad's sister, and she and my uncle were two of my favorite people in the world. After she walked around me several times and gave me numerous kisses, she asked, "Is that polyester your mom is wearing?" I looked her in the eyes with a wince and the two of us erupted in gales of laughter. My aunt and mother actually got along fairly well, but my mom's lack of dress sense had never escaped Aunt Marie's notice. I looked at my two relatives and thought to myself, *They are Vic and me twenty years from now. Forget twenty years from now. They're Vic and me* now!

Uncle Al was what you would call a "regular guy," just like my husband. He was friendly, intelligent, and funny, but, like Vic, he had the whole thrifty trait going for him. He and Vic could talk for hours about the cost-effectiveness of landscaping your own property versus having an outside contractor do it. One time, the two of them spent half a day trying to fix my twenty-year-old toaster before finally relenting and admitting that, yes, perhaps it really was time to buy a new toaster. To this day, they still dwelled on the delusion that if they had just tried a little harder, they probably could have had it up and running.

As usual, my brother-in-law, Pete, and his wife, Gabriella—or Gabby, as we all called her—were the last of the family to arrive. Actually, this was early for them, since they tended to always be late. Already steering himself in Neil's direction was my nephew, Jason, who was the same age as Neil. Both only children, they were more like brothers than like cousins. They also both had iPods in their hands and ear buds hanging around their necks. I assumed the decision had already been made that they would dislike the party music and would much rather listen to the one thousand plus songs on their iPods.

Just as I was debating going over and confiscating the antisocial devices, my sister-in-law, probably reading my mind, as she tended to do, grabbed my arm and exclaimed, "Ay yi yi! They drive me crazy too with those iPods, but just ignore them tonight, Jill! It's your night."

I turned and looked at Gabby with a resigned expression, and my mouth dropped open for the second time that night. I shut it quickly. Gabby was a very attractive Spanish woman with beautiful, long, straight black hair and big eyes to match, but forget the face. She was petite in height, with a drop-dead gorgeous body: huge breasts, flat stomach, firm butt, and shapely legs. If I didn't love her so much, I would hate her! Tonight she had on a skintight, red-hot red dress with a deep plunging V-neck, which was the reason for my jaw dropping. Holy cow! Those girls were just waiting to make an appearance! As usual, I felt a brief twinge of jealousy, but also, as usual, it passed. In actuality, my fifty-year-old sister-in-law was like a sister and best friend all rolled into one wonderful person, so I forced myself to overlook her "faults."

I then heard a lot of loud squeals and exclamations, and I turned on my zebra-shod feet and ran. My two other best friends were here, and the party could officially begin!

CHAPTER 3—NOW MEET
THE FRIENDS

"You look beautiful!" "Your hair looks great!" "Check out those shoes!" It went on and on as my three best friends oohed and aahed over one another while spinning around, flipping their hair, and striking poses. I was happy to see that a party at a VFW hall had done little to squash their desire to dress to the nines. Each one of them was unique-looking and, in my opinion, beautiful inside and out.

I had met all three women on the first day of seventh grade in what were a new school and a new town for me. They were together and already good friends. It was a tough town, so I wasn't sure when they approached me if they wanted to be friends or beat me up. Whatever the case, I was ready as I clenched my skinny fists behind my back. They walked over and introduced themselves. *OK, I thought. They don't care if I know who they are before they kick my butt.*

Instead, one girl, Patty, said, "I like your shirt."

The second girl, Barbara, bragged, "I have the same shirt at home in my closet."

The third, Kate, who up until this point had been looking me up and down, proceeded to pull out a bunch of small squares of colored construction paper stapled together and placed them near my face. For a second I thought she was going to assault me with paper, but instead, she shuffled through them until she found the color she wanted and said, "It's a great shirt, but burnt orange really isn't your color. I would go for a soft pink instead with your complexion." She then reached into her brown suede fringed bag and pulled out a compact mirror, showing me that I really did look better in pink.

From that day forward, pink would always be a staple color in my wardrobe. Most importantly, these three girls would become and remain my very best friends.

"Party! Party! Party!" they yelled in unison, followed by, "Drink! Drink! Drink!" With that, we all laughed hysterically as if we'd just been told the funniest joke. The four of us were easily amused and even more easily amused by one another. We were our own best audience.

At that moment, a huffing and puffing, heavy-set man, who I assumed to be the DJ because he was carrying a speaker, walked past us, and we once again broke out in gales of laughter. I had asked him to bring a disco ball as a reminder of our 1970s disco years. Well, Mr. DJ had decided to take it a step further. He appeared in an outfit that made him look like an overweight John Travolta in his *Saturday Night Fever* days. We're talking skin-tight white suit and slicked back hair.

Kate, between guffaws, spit out, "Did you request a Travolta look-alike?" and with that, she dashed off to the bathroom, holding her crotch and crying, "I can't take it!" Barb, Patty, and I were practically rolling on the floor as we watched her hasty exit! That was the second time today I had seen Kate's backside doing a jiggle. At least this time it was covered. I knew right there and then that this night was going to be one of the highlights of my life or, as we liked to refer to unique or special experiences, a "classic."

Where Kate was the outrageous one in our group, Patty was the most reserved. She could be just as silly as the rest of us, but when all was said and done, she was the mature, responsible one. She was our designated driver, our event planner, and the guide on our many adventures. We referred to her as the mother figure in the group. (Ironically, she was the only one of us who was unmarried and without children.) She said that someone had to take charge, and she didn't mind it being her. When any of us had a problem or an important decision to make, we always went to Patty first. We knew she would logically discuss the subject and even go so far as to pull out her ever-present notebook and write a list of pros and cons (or dos and don'ts).

I had always considered Barbara to be the one with the highest aspirations of our little foursome. When we were young, she was a bit of a bragger. If you or your family bought something new or cool, she claimed that she had the same or better at home. Rarely did we ever get to see these items, but we agreed that if having more than others was important to Barb, then who were we to burst her bubble? She still was a great person and a true-blue friend, so we just overlooked this particular short-coming. As I looked at her impeccable hair and dress, I thought that she really had done well for herself. She owned a very well-known real estate agency, she had married her college sweetheart, who was a Wall Street broker, and they had two great kids. The funny thing was that the more Barbara got in life, the less she bragged about it, until one day, without any of us actually recognizing the change, the bragging just ended. Even though Patty was the most mature friend, Barbara was the one who had truly "grown up."

As more family and friends continued to arrive, my three girlfriends took me by the arm and dragged me onto the dance floor as DJ Big Johnny T started the night off with, not surprisingly, "Night Fever"!

CHAPTER 4—PARTY!

"Jill! Jill! Hurry up! You have to see this!" came Barb's voice from the vestibule.

What could she want, I thought as I hurried over to her, with Patty and Kate right behind me. She stood there pointing to a stand in the lobby with a glass-enclosed announcement on it that said, "Happy 50th Birthday, Jill!"

"Oh, no!" I cried. "I gave the DJ and the VFW explicit instructions that there would be no mention of the word *fifty*!" We stood there for a few minutes, horrified and not quite sure what to do. We might *be* fifty, but we never actually acknowledged that fact in public. When we had turned forty, we made a pact that we would never admit to being a day over thirty-nine, thus remaining at that age forever. No one, not even our families, was allowed to tell our actual age, not *ever*!

Patty, always the quick thinker, said, "Kate! Pick that glass up!" Kate took one end, Barb took the other, and they lifted it up just far enough to get to the paper underneath that held the dreaded number. Patty then pulled White-Out (yes, she carried White-Out) from her pocketbook and, with a few quick swipes, permanently erased the offending number. The glass was eased back down, and we breathed a sigh of relief. Kate took out her camera and snapped a picture to record this moment for posterity.

Sometimes it just isn't easy being thirty-nine forever, I thought as we headed back inside.

At the party, we ate, drank, sang, danced, and laughed. Sometimes we laughed just for the sake of laughing. I looked at my three friends as we kicked and hopped to the Ramones like a bunch of jumping jelly beans with too much sugar added. One thing we all had in common was our height. We were a group of short people, from Barbara at five feet (or so she claimed—I had my doubts about that) to me (the tallest) at five feet three inches. Kate had shoulder-length, wavy brown hair, green eyes, and a medium build. When we were growing up, people always asked us if we were sisters. I supposed we still could pass as siblings. In direct contrast were Barbara and Patty. Barbara had short black hair, piercing black eyes, and a petite build. She was a little bottom-heavy, but guys loved her sashaying rear end. She may have been the shortest, but she possessed a very self-assured walk that sometimes made you think that she was taller. Single Patty was the blond-haired beauty of the group. With her long hair, clear blue eyes, and almost perfectly proportioned body, she was the one who always got the attention of the men around us. Even now, while jumping up and down like a bit of a fool, she managed to have this hair-swinging thing going on like she was in a commercial for a hair care product.

"The Hustle" came on, and Barbara grabbed me by both hands and started dancing. I could tell she was feeling good tonight. At one point, she gave me a butt bump (and what a butt to bump with), and I stumbled halfway across the dance floor. I took a bathroom break after that. When I headed back to the dance floor, I spotted Kate prodding Barbara back on too. Kate gave Barb a push, and Barb stumbled forward on her way to a header. It all happened in slow motion. I put out my arms. I really did try to catch her, but the next thing I knew, she was on the floor, her dress up around her waist, her round, bikini-clad bottom sticking up for the entire world to see! For the second time that night, Kate grabbed her crotch and ran hysterically to the bathroom. Barbara just bounced right back up like nothing unusual had happened and started dancing again. What a woman! Responsible Patty ran over to make sure that Barb was all right, but Barb just grabbed her by the hand and started dancing with her. I think as soon as Patty started running, all eyes probably turned toward her, so the "great fall," as it came to be referred to, was swiftly forgotten. We, of course, would always consider it a "classic" moment from the very "classic" party.

I happened to glance over at my nephew and son right after Barbara's floor dive. I noticed that Jason was bent over with laughter, but Neil had his head down with his hands over his face in what I assumed was sheer embarrassment. You'd think I was the one who fell. Apparently, it wasn't only his parents who mortified him, but also my best friends, whom he also thought of as his aunts.

Kate came out of the bathroom, having composed herself, and proceeded to march over to the table where our friends from Starbucks were sitting. My gaze went to the twelve 20-somethings whom Kate was attempting to lure to the dance floor. All of these "kids" (as we referred to them) worked at the local Starbucks where my friends and I met once a month for important girl time/talk. We'd been going there for about ten years and had seen many of them come and go. This group was the most recent, and we knew them well. Since I was at Starbucks on a daily basis, I tended to know them better than my friends did.

"Come on, guys! Let's dance! I'll dance with you! I'll dance with all of you!" I heard Kate exclaim as she pulled one of the guys with one hand and his girlfriend with the other. I had to give her credit, as within no time, she had all of them up and boogying.

The DJ was playing KC and the Sunshine Band, and my husband was shaking his "booty" hard to the song and looking quite comical in the process. Vic had been on the dance floor almost as much as us. He danced with anyone who was out there. Every once in a while, I spotted him in the middle of a circle, doing his thing. If you asked Vic if he liked to dance, he would tell you "no," but give him a few beers, and you couldn't hold him back. I suspected that tonight he had definitely consumed a "few" beers, but I didn't care. I was just happy to see him having such a great time! I chanced another quick look at Neil, and yes, he was once again in what would come to be his position for the evening: hands over face with head bent. At that point, I didn't know who was making me laugh harder, my husband or my son.

"Oh, Jill. When will you be serving the cake? People are looking for their dessert. What if they want to leave early?" My mother's voice brought me abruptly out of my merriment.

"Mom, I have an idea! Why don't *you* take care of the cake and let me enjoy *my* party?" I answered. She gave me a dirty look and turned, mumbling something about "speaking to Vic." If I knew my mother, she was probably the one looking to leave early. It was already past her bedtime. It would only be a matter of time before the kerchief was donned again, signaling her departure.

Gabby was pulling Papa onto the dance floor, and he had a huge smile on his face. Mama was still sitting in her seat. I didn't think she had gotten up all night, not even for a bathroom run. She had a serious look on her face, but I knew from experience that this didn't necessarily mean she wasn't having a good time. It was just how her face looked when she wasn't smiling. Although, maybe the fact that Papa was having a grand old time dancing *did* mean she wasn't a happy camper. For some unknown reason, she tended to get into a bad mood when her husband was having a better time than her.

Aunt Marie, with Uncle Al in tow, was playing her role as social butterfly. They and my dad were talking and laughing as my mom sat there with kerchief in hand, ready to bolt at the first opportunity. I knew that Aunt Marie would make the rounds, making sure that everyone was eating, drinking, and generally having a good time. I also knew that she did this not only because she genuinely enjoyed it but also because she wanted me to relax, have fun, and not have to worry that everyone else was properly fed and entertained. Have I said that she was one of my favorite people in the world?

All in all, it appeared that my guests were happy and the party was a success. I wished that I could have a party like this every year, but I seriously doubted my husband would go along with *that*! I had to give him credit, though. He and Neil had done a terrific job giving me a fiftieth birthday to remember, and for that I would always be grateful.

"I have a great idea!" I heard Kate's voice behind me, causing me to turn. "Why don't I invite Barb and Patty back to your house so we can celebrate all night?" With that, she ran off to inform the other girls of the plans and, I assumed, send her husband and son home without her.

Well, why not? It wasn't every day that a woman turned fifty. Now I just had to figure out where to send Vic and Neil. They wouldn't want to spend a night with four silly women. *Hmm*, I thought as I turned my gaze to the stern face of Mama Castillo.

CHAPTER 5—THE SLEEPOVER

By the time we got home, changed into comfy clothes, poured ourselves some wine, and got situated outside on my deck under the stars, it was one o'clock in the morning. We were tired, but too wound up from the party to sleep. I had even brought out some blankets and pillows in case we fell asleep on the deck. Kate passed around her camera so we could view the evening's pictures. The final one was taken by Vic at the end of the night; it was of the four of us leaning against a table, looking sweaty, flushed, mussed, and totally happy.

"That was the absolute best party I've ever been to," said Barbara. "Vic and Neil did an awesome job!" We nodded in agreement, then raised our glasses and yelled, "Hear, hear!" For the rest of the night, we rehashed every minute of the party, from who was there to what they were wearing and how they looked.

I was the last to fall asleep, so for a while I sat and gazed at my dear friends fondly. Through all of the years of parental, marital, familial, and even hormonal ups and downs, one thing always remained a constant, and that was our friendship. Yes, sometimes we encountered minor bumps in the road and got into arguments, but we always managed to make up and get past it. I think the older we became, the more we realized just how important our female friendships were, especially ones like ours that dated back to when we were kids. When one of us went through a high or low point in her life, so did the rest of us. We talked, laughed, and cried together. I supposed that the four of us were like a family.

When we turned thirty-nine, we agreed never to admit to being older, but we also made three other pacts. The first was that we would be there for one another forever. We knew that as people got older, many aspects of their lives could change, and not necessarily in a positive way, so we agreed that none of us would ever be left to handle life alone. The second decision was to meet once a month at Starbucks for catch-up time. This monthly meet ensured that the four of us would always be up-to-date on one another's lives. Only vacations or home and work emergencies were legitimate excuses to not attend. Lastly, we vowed to start exercising on a regular basis, preferably together if possible. This third pact proved to be the most difficult. In the beginning, we joined the same gym and designated certain nights for mandatory workouts. What we discovered was that, with job and family obligations, getting all of us together at the same time was too hard. We continued to exercise, but frequently there were only two of us there simultaneously. After about two years of gym membership, we decided that doing some type of a weekly class would be more doable and enjoyable for the group. To date, we've done jazzercise, yoga, Pilates, kickboxing (the most short-lived of the classes), and, our most recent and favorite, Zumba. It met twice a week at night, so there was always a class that we could attend.

As the girls snored on the deck, I thought back to that very first Zumba class and grinned. For starters, the four of us made up the rear of the class, so we could barely see what the instructor was doing. I was dressed in a sports bra, yoga pants, and a long-sleeved V-neck sweater. My intention had been to remove the sweater. Well, not a single other woman was working out in just a sports bra, so I was too embarrassed to take my sweater off. The end result was that halfway through the class, I was drenched in head-to-toe sweat, and by the end of the hour, I looked like I had gone for a vigorous swim.

Until Zumba, if asked, we all would have answered that we were pretty good dancers. Well, that first class totally ended our dancing self-esteem! The teacher turned one way and we turned the other. She jiggled her boobs and we wiggled our butts. She danced forward and we stumbled backward. Sometimes, we just stopped and stared at her or one another. Other times, we broke out into gales of laughter that earned us dirty looks from the instructor and our classmates. A year and a half later, we were Zumba-ing with much more finesse and experience than in that first class. We now stood in the front row, but we still were prone to fooling around and laughing, although our instructor was used to it now and usually laughed with us.

"Woof! Woof!" I turned and saw Oliver standing on the kitchen table, which was in front of the bay window that overlooked the deck. He did not look happy. I knew that he wanted to come outside with us to sleep, but if I let him out, he'd first jump all over Patty, Kate, and Barb, and then he'd settle down and everyone else would be wide awake and probably not very pleased. Oliver was a happy, perky, and energetic dog who loved everyone and wanted to be included in everything, but tonight I thought his over-exuberance might not be greeted well.

I guess sleep eventually overcame me, as I was awakened by a loud grunt followed by an exclamation of "*Shit!* What the hell happened to my body?" from Kate. I opened my eyes and saw that she was hunched over and attempting to walk—and not very successfully, I might add. She made it about three feet, then collapsed onto a bench and lay back down, groaning.

Patty and Barb opened their eyes and stared at her without saying anything. They, too, tried to get up. Patty, who had drunk the least, seemed to be moving nimbly, but Barb was stumbling and groaning like Kate. "I guess it's times like this when we really feel our age," she said.

Kate sat up, saying, "Screw fifty! I feel like I'm ninety! What the hell did we do to feel this bad? I know we danced a lot, but aren't we supposed to be in dancing shape from Zumba? I'm calling our instructor and demanding an eighteen-month refund!"

I would have agreed with her except that my mouth seemed to be stuffed with cotton balls. Since speaking was out of the question, I grunted. I remembered our twenties, when we could drink, dance, come home at four in the morning, sleep a few hours, and then go back out again and party more. From the looks of us now, we would need a good week to recuperate from last night.

We decided that some good, strong coffee was much needed, so we dressed and headed to "our" Starbucks just as Vic and Neil were coming home. Neither of them said anything other than "Good morning," but from the looks on their faces, I knew they'd be laughing hard as soon as we closed the door.

We ordered our coffees, settled down on our favorite couches, and drank happily and peacefully for the first fifteen minutes. Kate, as usual, was the first to speak. Barb, Patty, and I could have sat there all morning and not uttered a word, but it was rare for Kate to sit quietly.

"I've been giving this a lot of thought," she said as we blearily looked at her through still-swollen eyes. "As of Patty's birthday in the middle of September, we'll all be fifty."

"*Shh!*" the three of us said in unison, hastily looking around to see if anyone had heard.

"Oops! Sorry," said Kate, but continued. "We're all due for our you-know-what-age colonoscopies, and I have an idea. Why don't we all go together? I'm thinking that we can schedule them one right after the other. It will be true solidarity. You know, it would be something like 'friends who cleanse together stay together.' Speaking of cleansing together, we should hopefully drop a few pounds! Maybe we could even skip Zumba that week!"

Barb said, "Wherever do you get your insane ideas?"

I said, "I'll do anything to lose weight!"

Patty pulled out her ever-handy planner and started reciting dates that she was available. After some discussion, the decision was unanimously made; Kate, Barb, Patty, and I were going to have a girls' colonoscopy day.

It was going to be a "blast!"

CHAPTER 6—GROUP COLONOSCOPY

A month later, the big day was almost here. We had our appointments in twenty-minute intervals commencing at 9 a.m. The goal was to be done by noon so we could eat lunch afterward. We knew that we would be very hungry after a day and a half of virtual starvation.

The night before the big test, we conference-called one another for "colonoscopy prep" support. Mostly the support was for Kate because she was gagger. Ever since we were kids, if she ate or drank something that she disliked, she immediately started gagging and would either spit the ingested substance into a napkin or run to the bathroom to vomit. It wasn't a pretty sight, but by now we were immune to it.

On the count of three, we were to down the prep

drink. Sure enough, we heard, "Argh! Aarg! Yuck! Yuck! Agh!" followed by very loud gagging. I was also gagging, so I wasn't going to be much help, apparently.

I heard Barb yell over the unpleasant sound, "Would you just drink it up quick, Kate? You have to do it, so *do IT*! If you don't, I swear I'll come over and pour it down your throat!"

I laughed as I imagined five-foot-nothing Barb sitting on Kate and pouring the noxious liquid into her mouth while Kate gagged it back up into Barb's face. Patty must have been having similar visions because over all the noise, I could still hear her laughing and snorting. From looking at Patty, you would never guess that those unattractive sounds could come out of such an attractive woman, but just as Kate was a gagger, Patty was a snorter. It was so funny, it made us laugh even harder.

"Come on, you guys," Barb pleaded. "We have to do this, and we have a long way to go."

Eventually, all of us got the first glass down, and by later that evening and the next morning, there were no more phone calls. The four of us were glued to our respective toilet bowls. I sat on my own toilet and stared aimlessly at the bathroom walls, then started reminiscing. It wasn't as if I had anything better to do anyway.

I thought back to our grammar school days, specifically seventh and eighth grade. We were an immature group of girls. Well, in all honesty, we still were. Every day was the start of a new adventure for us. Other kids dreaded going to school, but we loved it. We got into a lot of trouble, but nothing mean-spirited, just kid trouble. Kate and I wore braces back then, and I mean *braces*: the old, ugly kind that glittered and sparkled like a tinsel-adorned Christmas tree. We had these tiny rubber bands on them, and during class we would take them off (we always kept a fresh supply on hand) and shoot them at the back of the boys' heads. They'd start grabbing their heads, and Kate, Barb, Patty, and I would have to put our faces behind our books because we were laughing so hard. Needless to say, our stern, elderly teacher would punish us for disrupting the class, although she didn't know about the rubber bands. It still amazed me that we'd done this for an entire school year and the boys never discovered what it was that was pinging their heads.

We also tormented the boys during music class. Our teacher educated us in various ethnic dances, and dancing to "Hava Nagila" was the most fun. The boys formed the inner circle, while the girls created an outside one. Every time the song required a kick, we would kick the boys in the butt. I supposed, in retrospect, that our teacher was a very tolerant woman, as she never reprimanded us for our antics.

Our worst prank was probably the ice cubes. Kate lived on the third floor of an apartment building. The four of us would meet there after dark. This was a nighttime stunt. There were two boys a year younger than us who were always walking up and down the street. Both of them were cute, but one of them we didn't like. We would keep the living room light off and arm ourselves with ice cubes. When the boys passed by, we would throw the cubes at them. They'd stand there, looking around to see who had thrown something at them and from where. Since we were on the third floor and the windows were dark, the boys couldn't see us. This went on almost every day for a school year. One day, Barb and Patty weren't able to come over, so it was just Kate and me throwing the ice. Well, the boys spotted us and ran into her building. I went out into the hallway to see where they were and was almost confronted by two very angry boys who were rounding the landing fast and heading my way. Kate was standing in her doorway, and with some sort of Herculean power, she reached forward, grabbed me by the collar, pulled me in the doorway, and then slammed and locked the door before the boys could get to us. To this day, I have no idea how she did that. The boys pounded on the door, finally giving up and leaving, and Kate and I never got in trouble. We *did* stop throwing the ice cubes after that terrifying night, but we were always able to find other, less dangerous ways to tease boys. As I said, we were quite immature and didn't really start maturing (well, a little bit) until our sophomore year in high school.

As I sat there on my toilet bowl, I thought back to our seventh grade bathroom pranks. The four of us would arrange to meet in the girls' room, usually at lunchtime. We would crowd into the janitor's supply closet and somehow situate ourselves on and around the boxes and brooms. The eighth-grade girls would come in, and we would listen to the latest gossip if we kept the door slightly ajar. For some reason, this gave us extreme pleasure to overhear, even if sometimes we had no idea what or whom they were talking about. One boring, uneventful bathroom day, we were in our usual spots and ready to call it quits when in walked a teacher. Teachers *never* used the girls' room, as they had their own private bathroom. This teacher went into a stall and pulled down what sounded to us like rubber underpants. (I still have no idea what they actually were.) At that point, while hysteria was bubbling up in us and threatening to overflow, she let out a loud fart! Well, that was our undoing! The four of us practically fell off our seats we were laughing so hard, and then we were on our feet, stumbling and out the door before whoever was in the stall could pull up her rubber pants and chase us down. As with the ice cube debacle, it was the last time we ever played bathroom hideout again!

I was brought back to the present by Vic's voice. "Are you ever coming out of there? I need to take a shower!" Vic had been kind enough to go in to work late so he could drive us to our test, and my sister-in-law, Gabby, was picking us up.

"OK! OK!" I yelled back. I supposed that daydreaming time was over; beside, at this point there was nothing left in me to come out.

Barb, Kate, Patty, and I walked into the colonoscopy center a short time later, literally drained. We were totally exhausted from being in our bathrooms a good part of the night and early morning. None of us wore make-up, and we were all dressed in sweats. It was not a pretty sight.

"OK, girls, this is the big day," announced Kate, who always managed to muster up some degree of perkiness no matter how bad she felt. I wanted to throttle her, but I didn't have the strength. Barb and Patty gave her a dirty look and collapsed onto a couch. Poor Patty. This was one of those rare times that even *she* didn't look good.

Barb stood, saying, "All I can say is that I hope my butt got smaller from this torture," and did a swaying twirl. We all agreed that indeed her butt did look smaller. "I lost two pounds!" she added, and we responded with weak but supportive claps.

Kate said that she also had lost two, and Patty claimed to have dropped one, which earned them tired applause too.

"I didn't lose an ounce!" I cried. "How is that possible? I can't believe I went through all of *that* for nothing!"

"Well, Jill," said the ever-practical Patty, "You're really doing this for health reasons and not for weight loss."

"Easy for you to say!" I replied, my voice rising. "You lost a pound!"

We were spent, grumpy, and downright bitchy. Just as the situation was beginning to escalate, a nurse came out and said, "Hello, ladies! I've been told that you're having the procedure one after another, so you might as well come in the back together and get undressed." With that, we calmed down and marched in a line to meet our Maker. That's what it felt like, at least. Having a colonoscopy must be some earthly test that one must pass before moving on to bigger and better things. I was of the opinion that since women had to go through years of menstruation, with the added agony of childbirth thrown in, we should be given a free pass on colonoscopies. Apparently, however, that was not going to happen.

By noon, we were done and standing in the waiting

room, anticipating my sister-in-law's arrival. I looked at Kate, Patty, and Barb's faces and saw that they were feeling as groggy as I was, but there was something unexpected, also. Their faces were wearing a goofy look! *Do I look like that too?* I wondered. My thought was answered a minute later as we suddenly started laughing in unison, even though no one had uttered a word.

"What the hell did they give us?" laughed Patty.

"This is good stuff!" said Barb.

"Woo-hoo!" said Kate, then bent over in a giggling fit.

Naturally I joined in, and the next thing I knew, we were all giggling. Well, actually, Patty was doing some kind of snorting giggle. The other patients in the waiting room were giving us strange, somewhat fearful glances, so I ushered the girls outside.

Gabriella pulled up at that exact moment, took one look at us, and exclaimed, "Ay yi yi! What have you girls been drinking?" which caused more fits of hysteria. "Ay yi yi!" was Gabby's favorite expression, and she used it as a response to a whole gamut of incidences. "Since when is a colonoscopy so much fun? Now I wish I'd gone too," she added. Admittedly, it didn't take much to set us off, but whatever the docs had given us for sedation seemed to be having a silly effect on us.

Afterward, the five of us went to Starbucks, as we were not only hungry but also coffee-deprived. Eventually the giddiness wore off, and we looked similar to when we first arrived for our test early this morning: tired and "drained."

We celebrated the end of the colonoscopies and our

good results by gorging on high-fat and high-calorie lattes, egg sandwiches, and desserts. What the hell! It was not every day that you got a colonoscopy! There was always tomorrow to drop those extra pounds.

Or maybe next week…

CHAPTER 7—HOT FLASH?

I awakened one August morning not feeling well. I was tired and warm and thought that perhaps I was getting sick. Vic was already up when I came downstairs. He took one look at me and said, "What's the matter, Jill? You look sick, and your face is red." With that, he reached out and touched my forehead. "You're warm, too. Maybe you should stay home and relax today." I shook my head no. The girls were going out to dinner, and it was rare that that we could coordinate a Saturday night outing. I figured that I could take it easy this after-noon, and hopefully I'd feel better this evening.

As the day wore on, I felt markedly improved and chalked the bad morning up to allergies. By six-thirty, I was showered, dressed, and out the door. Patty picked me up, and we headed to a new local Italian restaurant to meet Kate and Barb. This was the first time that all of us would be getting together since our colonoscopy extravaganza, so there was a lot to talk about. Kate's son, Lou Jr., and Neil were leaving for college in a week, so tonight was something of a support group dinner for Kate and me.

As usual, we greeted one another as if we hadn't been together in months: with lots of squeals, hugs, and kisses. Finally, we were settled down at a table and our wine order had been placed. Patty and Barb started right off commiserating with Kate and me over the impending, depressing departure of our sons and only children. Barb also had sons. One was twenty and still in the process of deciding what he wanted to be when he "grew up," and the youngest was going to be a high school senior. A year from now, we would be replaying this scenario to commiserate with her. Since Patty had no children, she treated our sons as if they were her own. Sometimes I suspected that Neil told her "secrets" that he didn't tell me. She was like a friend and mom rolled into one. I was fine with that, as I knew that if it was anything of importance, she would relay it to me (without his knowledge, of course).

In another week, we had plans to get together again for the "day the boys are leaving" crying free-for-all. Tonight Kate and I were still able to smile and laugh, but next week would be a real bawling-fest! I could picture us, glasses of wine in hand, sobbing uncontrollably. Patty had already invited us over to her condo, since we didn't think going out would be such a good idea. If Kate and I got too blubbery and drunk, we could simply crash in Patty's guest bedroom. The upside to next weekend was that we wouldn't have to wear make-up, and *that* was always a good thing!

As Patty, Barb, and Kate were discussing a movie that they had recently seen, I started feeling funny. Not funny as in "ha-ha" but funny as in strange in the head. I looked at my wine glass and saw that I had only drunk a half of a glass, so it wasn't the wine. My face felt red-hot, and my brain was confused. I could no longer follow their conversation! What the hell was going on? The next thing I knew, I couldn't breathe and my heart was racing!

"Uh! Girls! Something's wrong," I whispered. They were now in the midst of debating whether or not a particular movie deserved to be Academy-Awarded, and therefore ignored me. "Patty!" I yelled (since she *was* the most responsible one). "I think I'm having a heart attack!"

Kate choked on her wine. Barb jumped up and started slapping me on the back! *What the hell was that all about?* Patty, very calmly, pulled out her cell phone and dialed 911.

"I don't want to go to the hospital!" I cried. I looked at Patty. "Remember my instructions!" I said. Over the course of the last few years, I had given Patty instructions as to what she should immediately remove from among my belongings upon my demise. One of these items was a (never used, I swear) vibrator in one of my dresser drawers that Vic had given me about ten years ago. I shuddered to think of the long-term psychological effects on Neil should he discover *that* instrument! Given how responsible Patty was, I totally trusted her to carry out the task. Had I asked Kate, she would have run around the house laughing and waving it in the air. Barb, who was a tad bit sentimental, would have probably glass-enclosed it with a "Tribute to Jill" plaque on the front.

The ambulance came, and I was embarrassingly loaded onto a gurney and driven to the hospital, my girl-friends following close behind. I was now breathing easi-er and seriously considering making a mad break for it. I stared at the closed ambulance doors. *If I jumped up quickly and with one fluid motion opened the doors and jumped (like they did in the movies), I could escape!* What was I thinking? This was not a movie or a book. This was real life. *Maybe I could bribe the ambulance guys to let me out at the next corner and pretend that I had escaped.* Nah! I didn't think that would work either. I closed my eyes and steeled myself for further embar-rassment.

As I was being unloaded, Kate jumped out of Patty's car, crying and screaming, "Jill! I love you! Please don't leave me!"

Shit, I thought. Could it get any worse? Well, appar-ently it could. I was rushed into the hospital with some-one yelling, "Code _____!" I couldn't really make out what they were saying, but at least it wasn't "code blue," so I relaxed.

After blood work, a chest X-ray, an EKG, and an echocardiogram, I was rolled into a curtain-enclosed cu-bicle in the emergency room, where my three teary-eyed friends were waiting. At that point, I felt much better and decided to get up, dress, and leave the hospital. Patty was

having none of that though. She pushed me right back
down and told me, "Stay still!" as she left to find my doctor.

Well, my doctor turned out to be a thirty-something-
year-old, blond, surfer-looking dude. Not my type, but
still very cute in a surfer-dude kind of way. I immediately
lay back down and started moaning. It wasn't every day
that a thirty-nine-year-old got this kind of male attention,
and I intended on milking it! Out of the corner of my eye,
I saw Barb eyeing me warily, but I chose to ignore her.

"Doc," I said, "I think I may need a physical." "Doc"
leaned over me, and Patty snorted. Damn her for always
trying to steal the attention! Patty's snort apparently was
contagious, because Barb and Kate were laughing very
loud and "Doc" was also beginning to look amused.

After the laughter had died down, the doctor asked,
"Mrs. Castillo, is it correct that you are fifty years old?"

Crap! Nabbed! "If you say so, Doctor," I replied innocently.

"Before the breathing difficulty and rapid heartbeat,
what were your exact symptoms?" he asked. I told him
what had happened, to which he replied, "Well, Mrs.
Castillo, all of your tests have come back normal. When
was your last period?" *Is he crazy? What does my period
have to do with a heart attack?* I lay there thinking back,
way back, and then answered, "I think it was about a year
ago."

He leaned over and very seriously looked me straight
in the eyes, and I gulped. His next words floored me, and
apparently those around me, when he said, "Part of what
occurred was an anxiety attack, but what I do believe

you've had is a hot flash. It's really quite normal at your age."

I had no idea what he said after that because his words were drowned out by my best friends' raucous laughter!

CHAPTER 8—OUR BABIES ARE LEAVING US

Exactly one week after the hospital fiasco, we were back together, ensconced in our favorite comfy clothes, make-up-less, our hair in ponytails, and sprawled out in Patty's living room.

She had outdone herself with the comfort-food spread. Besides the mandatory bottles of wine, uncorked and ready to be poured, there was a variety of fattening foods on display. She had filled a popcorn bowl with those cute mini chocolate treats that stores sell during holidays: Snickers, Reese's peanut butter cups, and Godiva dark chocolate truffles! What woman doesn't need dark chocolate in her hour of need—and Godiva, no less! There were potato chips with onion dip, nachos with salsa, and Cheetos! I had to force myself to look away from the coffee table before I passed out right on top of those delectable treats!

Kate reached down into a large tote bag next to her chair and pulled out photo albums. I leaned closer to see while asking, "Hey, Kate! What's with all the pictures?"

She immediately began bawling. "They're Lou's baby pics! Oh, Jill! I'm going to miss him *so* much!" She whipped out a box of tissues from the tote, opened it, and blew loudly. I half expected her to reach back down and pull Lou Jr. out of there too!

Barb started crying and I looked at her. "Why are you crying, Barb? Your son doesn't leave for college for another year!"

"I know!" she sobbed. "I really don't know why I'm crying!"

Patty walked over to her desk, grabbed some sheets of paper, and held them up. "Kate! Look!" she said. "I printed out Lou's schedule of classes! I have Neil's too, Jill! Now you two will always know where they are during the week!"

Kate cried even harder. "Lou's going to college in Colorado! Wah! I won't see him until Thanksgiving!" With that, she got up, grabbed her tissue box, and ran into the bathroom. I guessed that she didn't think Patty owned any tissues, or maybe she just wasn't taking any chances.

I didn't need to bring baby photos to picture Neil when he was young. His beautiful little round face would always be indelibly stamped in my mind along with his black hair and black eyes. He had been the picture of perfection when he was born! In my eyes, he still was. I took some measure of comfort in knowing that his school was less than an hour away, but still I was going to miss him terribly. I had given up my career to stay home and raise him, and I didn't regret it for an instant, but I already was starting to feel lonely. Yes, I had Vic and my friends, but it wasn't the same. Kate and I still thought of our sons as our babies, and our babies were leaving!

Oh no! It hit me then, and I cried out, "My baby is leaving me! What if he never comes home to live? What if he meets a girl from another state and wants to move there? You know a boy will always follow the girl! What if I have to move to some state far away? I'll miss you guys so much!" I was out of control, and I couldn't get a grip on myself as I was inundated with all of these terrible thoughts.

Right at that moment, my cell phone rang. I was blubbering so much that Patty had to answer it for me. After a minute of speaking to the caller, she turned to me. "Jill, Neil wants to know where his underwear is." She put the phone to her ear again and then added, "Oh, and he says can you come home early tomorrow because he doesn't know how to pack his suitcase?" With the consoling thought that my baby still needed me, I stopped crying and ate a chocolate bar in two bites. They don't call it comfort food for nothing.

Kate came out of the bathroom shortly thereafter, and we settled down for a long night of eating, drinking, and, most importantly, talking. We didn't speak any further about our kids' leaving. We'd deal with that tomorrow. The rest of the night became about us.

Every once in a while, Patty's phone would vibrate

and she'd start texting someone, but there was something odd about her face when it happened. I sensed secrecy, which was a rare occurrence in this group. Hmm. "Oh, Patty. Who is it that keeps texting you?"

She looked up at me with her make-up-less but still beautiful face and said innocently, "It's just my mom. She's doing some redecorating and wants my opinion."

I didn't say anything further, but frankly, I didn't for one minute believe her. Something was going on! I had this wild urge to dive across the table and grab her phone, but I suppressed it for now. She must have sensed that I was on to her because she stopped texting after that. I guess her mother was done redecorating. *Yeah, right!*

Kate and Barb, who had been chatting in the kitchen while replenishing the snacks, came back in, so I let the texting subject drop.

"How have you been feeling since the hot flash, Jill?" asked Kate. "You really scared us. I heard that hot flashes are bad, but not *that* bad! You looked a little like an overripe tomato about to burst! I kept waiting for the explosion. Oops! Sorry," she said when she saw the expression on my face. "I didn't mean to be insensitive!" Leave it to Kate to bring humor to what was really not a humorous experience. Kate's question then led to a discussion on menopause.

"That was the worst feeling!" I answered. "One minute I was fine, and the next, it was like my face was on fire, but the fire was on the inside of my skin. I've had them every day at eleven o'clock at night since Saturday. Go figure! I have to run outside to cool off. It stinks! Every time I run out, Oliver thinks he has to go out too, so it's becoming a nuisance, to say the least. On top of that, I haven't slept all week because I keep getting warm all night. *Ugh!* I'm too hot, then I take off my covers and I'm too cold, and then I put the covers back on and I'm hot again! I put the central air on sixty-four degrees, and I swear that Vic started twitching when he saw what it was set on. When I left the room, he must have pushed it back up to seventy because I was sweating my butt off. I just *know* that this is going to be a problem. I can see us getting a divorce over the air temperature. How long is this menopause stuff going to last?" I chugged my glass of wine in an unladylike way.

My friends sat there staring at me for a few minutes, and then Kate said, "Gee, you're really worked up about this, aren't you, Jill?"

"I'm not worked up!" I yelled at her. "I'm too damn hot!"

Patty quickly handed me another glass of wine, and I calmed down. "I'm sorry, Kate. It's really not that bad. I just hate feeling warm all the time. On the positive side, I haven't had my period in over a year, and I'm loving that!"

Barb looked deep in thought, and then she said, "I think Jerry is going through some kind of male menopause." Jerry was Barb's husband. "He's been moody for months, and he keeps staring at himself in the mirror and obsessing over his gray hair."

Kate chuckled. "Lou does the same thing, and he seems to be working out more and more like he's trying to stop his body from aging. Don't say anything to him, but he *does* have love handles!"

We were all giggling now. "Vic does too." I said. "He says he has less hair where he wants it and more where he doesn't!"

"I'm starting to forget words," said Patty. "The other day I couldn't remember the word *iron*! I mean seriously ladies... *iron*! How simple is that?"

"I can beat that!" I said. "Two weeks ago when Vic and I were driving to his coworker's barbeque, some jerk started beeping at us because we weren't going fast enough, and I yelled out to him to stop *barking*!"

"Hysterical!" laughed Patty. "What did he say?"

"Oh, he didn't say anything." I answered. "My window was closed, so he didn't hear me, but Vic did, and I thought he was going to crash the car because he was laughing so hard!"

Barb screamed, "I've got a good one! How about when you walk into a room and you have no idea what you went in there for? Then when you leave, you remember what you wanted, and you go back and forget *again*! It drives me crazy!"

Organized Patty added, "I've taken to leaving Post-It notes everywhere, even in my pocketbook and in my car!"

I said, "I'll leave stuff by the basement and attic stairs just to remind me to bring them up or down, even if I don't have to do it until the next day. I'm so afraid that I'm going to forget! Sometimes I do random things like leaving a cabinet open to remind me to do something totally unrelated like taking the clothes out of the washer. It's crazy, I know, but it helps!"

"Hey! Do you guys go to the bathroom a lot?" We

stopped laughing and looked at Kate. No one that I've ever met went to the bathroom as much as Kate did.

"Kate? Is it even possible for you to go more?" I said. "How would you even notice if you did?"

"Well," she said. "I used to go every thirty minutes, and now I go every twenty minutes. Don't stare at me like that! I know that you three go a lot, too!" She was right. It did seem that no sooner was I done peeing than I was rushing back to the bathroom to go again. I may not be going every twenty minutes like Kate, but my output definitely was increasing.

With that, the four of us decided that all of this bathroom talk had given us the need to pee, so we decided to take a short bathroom break. As Kate hurried to be first in line (as usual), she said, "Men have it so easy! Besides some minor hair concerns and love-handle issues, getting older is *so* easy for them. Plus, they still get to pee standing up!" Leave it to Kate to sum things up neatly and humorously.

When we were settled down again, this time with pillows and blankets, we decided to put on a movie. Before long, my eyes were closing, and I could see through the slits that so were Barb, Patty, and Kate's. What I originally thought was going to be a sad, tear-filled night centering on the boys' forthcoming college departure had turned into a relaxing and entertaining evening. As I've contemplated so many times before, whatever would I do without my girlfriends? And with that calming thought, I fell fast asleep.

CHAPTER 9—MOVING DAY

No sooner had I walked in the door on Sunday morning with a hangover and a splitting headache than Neil was upon me with last-minute questions. "Where is the splitter for the cable? Did you pack an extension cord? Do you think we have enough water and Gatorade?" Yowza! The questions were endless, so I did what any good mother would do: I ran to the bathroom and shut and locked the door in his face. "Mom! Are you going to help me?"

I looked around the bathroom for someplace to hide. Hmm. Could I fit in the cabinet under the vanity? That was where the toilet paper and tissues were kept, and since he never put out fresh toilet products when they were needed, he'd never find me there. I didn't think I could fit, but I could do what Oliver did when he wanted to hide: put my head in and make believe that people couldn't see my butt sticking out. Nope, that wasn't going to work either. My butt was much bigger than Oliver's. Crap! I was going to have to open the door, so I took aspirin and a deep breath and opened the door to an exasperated Neil.

"Come on, kiddo. The answer to all of your questions is yes, so let's get your stuff in the car."

The doorbell rang, and in walked my brother. *Why is it that no one ever waits for me to answer the door? What if Vic and I were dancing around naked or, heaven forbid, being intimate?* I shuddered at the thought of my brother or Mama Castillo walking in on that scene.

"Jill? Why are you standing there violently shaking your head?" asked Vic as he passed me with suitcases in hand. He continued on his way, so I guessed he didn't really expect an answer.

"Hey, Jill! Check out what I invented for Neil for his college move-in!" Anthony walked in pushing some large, bulky object.

Oh no! I cringed. Another of Ant's ghastly inventions! My brother was smiling from ear to ear as he gave me the rundown on his thingamajig, for lack of a better word. It was a dolly, but not just a dolly. He had welded two shelves to it, with hooks sticking out of the sides of the shelves. The part of the dolly closest to his body had what appeared to be a canvas laundry bag tied to the top and bottom. The device was huge and looked like it weighed a ton. He showed me how you could shelve your suitcases and flat items while hanging shopping bags on the sides and storing loose items in the front sack.

"You'll be able to move everything in one organized trip!" he exclaimed excitedly.

Quite frankly, I didn't know what to say. Anthony could be very sensitive about his inventions. I remembered when he created the doggie skateboard. He had demonstrated the fun that Oliver could have by strapping my dog's paws onto the skateboard and giving him a gentle push. *Plop* went poor Oliver as he fell to the side with the board still attached to him. Ant righted him again and gave him another push resulting in another *plop*! I had laughed so hard that my brother didn't talk to me for a week after that! Now that I thought about it, that had been a very peaceful week.

I was brought out of my musings by Vic's voice. "What the hell is that *thing*?" I tried very hard not to laugh at his expression, although even I had to admit that Ant had outdone himself on this one! I kept expecting the thing to start rolling and talking like the robot from the old show *Lost in Space*. Maybe it would start waving its shelves too! Oh no! I was going to lose it, so I ran toward the front door and smacked into Mama Castillo.

She gave me the dirtiest look, as if I had run into her on purpose. She walked past me with Papa following like the good husband that he was, and then she screamed loudly, "Mama mia! Qué es esto?" I assumed she had just met Anthony's latest invention.

Wow! So this is what it took to scare my mother-in-law! I liked this dolly thingy more and more! I envisioned leaving it right by the front door, forever terminating her unannounced visits!

As I turned to follow my in-laws, Pete, Gabby, and Jason walked in! I really needed to start locking my door! "Come on in," I said, "and join the crowd."

I could probably have sneaked out right then and no one would have been the wiser, but it was too late. Gabby was already pulling me toward the kitchen, saying, "We just wanted to come and say good-bye to Neil and see if you needed any help. Pete said he didn't know if you were going to be able to fit everything in your car." Gabby entered the kitchen and stopped in her tracks. "Ay yi yi! What is that thing and what are you doing to poor Oliver?" Sure enough, Anthony was wheeling a barking Oliver around the kitchen. I couldn't tell if Oliver was shaking from fear or excitement. Just in case it was fear, I hurried over and scooped him up off the dolly.

My mother-in-law had Neil in a body lock as she squeezed him and cried, "Adiós, mi pobre niño! Adiós!" Mama had been calling Neil and Jason "pobres niños" since the day they were born. I sincerely doubted that either grandson was a "poor boy." She hugged my son, and Papa slipped money into his hand, as he always did when he saw his grandchildren. He must have realized that he hadn't given Jason money too, so he hurried over to my nephew and quickly gave him a few bills. My in-laws always made sure that their grandchildren were given the exact same amount of money lest one of them feel deprived. After almost eighteen years of these gifts, my dear son had more money than I did!

The result of their generosity was that whenever I pushed him to get a j-o-b, he would always say, "Why do I need a job, Mom? I have plenty of money!" I kept hop-

ing that one of these days Papa would slip me some of
those bills, but so far that hadn't happened, and if Mama
had any say, it never would. Again, I thought about the
benefits of leaving that dolly in my foyer, but then I
sighed. Vic probably wouldn't let me, and anyway, after
this morning's adventure, Oliver would probably freak
out and be scarred for life if we kept it here.

My head was still pounding (so much for the aspirin)
as I glanced at the clock. Holy cow! We had only half an
hour to get out of here, and my house looked like there
was a party going on! Mama was putting out a pot of coffee, and Gabby had placed scones and pastries on a plate.
I hadn't even had the time to take a shower since returning from Patty's house. As I looked around, I wished that
I was back at Patty's cozy, noiseless, family-less condo.

The telephone was ringing, and either everyone was
deaf or they couldn't be bothered to pick it up. I was used
to both since neither Vic nor Neil ever answered the
phone. They could be standing right next to it and totally
ignore the ringing. Like father, like son. They didn't even
answer it when I wasn't home. When I complained about
it, my guys would give me the same lame excuses: "It's
always for you, so why should we answer it?" or "Let the
answering machine pick it up." Yes, most of the time the
calls were for me, but it was still annoying.

Now *everyone* in my kitchen seemed to be boycott-
ing the telephone, so I pushed my way through the throng
to get it. It was my sister, Kelly, calling to wish Neil good
luck. Unlike the rest of the family, Kelly would *never*
stop by unannounced. She was the epitome of prim and
proper, which could sometimes be unnerving but in this

instance was very much appreciated. I didn't think I could handle one more guest!

"Jill, what is all that noise?" asked Kelly. Before I could explain the situation, she continued, "Is that Anthony's voice? Are you having a farewell party? Who else is there? I can't believe you didn't tell me!" As I started to explain the impromptu party, the doorbell rang.

Who was it now? I had about ten seconds to think before my mother and father walked in! Were they kidding me? Had the entire family gone crazy? Maybe I was still sleeping at Patty's house, and this was all just a bad dream.

Nope! No such luck! My mother's voice rang out too loud and too clear to be a dream, and she brushed past me while pulling off her bright pink kerchief that matched her even brighter pink sweatshirt. With the white sweatpants, she looked like a vanilla and strawberry milkshake.

"Jill! Why are all of these people here? And Anthony, whatever is *that* contraption?" Leave it to Mom to come up with the perfect word.

"Well, Mom, why are you here?" I asked.

"Oh, I see," she said. "It's OK for the rest of the family to come and wish my grandson good luck in college, but I'm imposing if I want to do the same. Why do you always have to start a fight with me, Jill?"

Before I could retort, Dad came to the rescue. "Now, Gloria, I don't think Jill was picking a fight with you. I think she just meant that everyone else is here for the same reason that we are. Right, Jill?"

I just nodded. My head was hurting so badly that my mother's voice was still ricocheting back and forth inside it. I placed my hand over my eyes to block out the light *and* my mother's face as Aunt Marie walked up behind me, saying, "Jill, honey, are you feeling ill? Maybe you should go lie down for a few minutes."

"Good idea, Aunt Marie! Can you hold down the fort for ten?"

"Sure. Your uncle and I just wanted to give this coffee pot to Neil to bring with him. You know how those college kids need their caffeine when they're pulling all-nighters!"

"Jill? Jill!" Kelly's voice rang out. Crap! I'd totally forgotten that my sister was still on the phone, so instead of answering her, I handed the receiver over to Mom and left her to placate her younger daughter.

I slipped away from the commotion and laughed about the coffee pot. My aunt and I shared a common love of and addiction to new coffee systems, which drove Uncle Al and Vic crazy. It didn't matter if our "old" coffee pots worked fine. We could never resist the impulse to purchase a new and improved one. And since we could never part with our old pots, we both had cabinets full of gently used coffee pots. I assumed that Aunt Marie had felt the need to buy another. So as to not start an argument with my uncle, she was giving it to Neil, thereby satisfying her necessity to make the purchase. I didn't have the heart to tell her that Neil didn't drink coffee, and I hoped my son would refrain from telling her. He could always wrap it up for Christmas and give it back to her as a gift, which would make her very happy. Or I could keep it and make myself very happy. It was a win-win situation.

Now that I had given myself a couple of private chuckles and relaxed a bit, I was ready to face my unexpected company. Thanks to my aunt, my headache was dissipating, so I got up, marched into the kitchen, clapped my hands, and said, "Everyone out now, and I mean *now*! And Ant, take your contraption with you! It's too heavy, and it's never going to fit in the car!"

While muttering, grumbling, and bidding hasty farewells, the family filed out the front door, with a forlorn Ant and his dolly bringing up the rear like a caboose that had lost the rest of the train.

Fifteen minutes later, Neil, Vic, and I had the car packed up and were en route to the college where we would leave our only child for the next four years. And with that thought, I began to cry.

CHAPTER 10—AS ONE MAN LEAVES, ANOTHER ENTERS

I now understood what the term *empty nest syndrome* meant, and I didn't like it, although so far Vic seemed to be faring much better than me. The house was too quiet. There was no laundry to do or groceries to buy or socks to pick up. There was no one to boss around. There was no one to grunt at me or ignore me when I talked. OK, not entirely true. There was still Vic, but it was different. I wanted to hear Neil's grunts. I'd been crying for almost a month. I hadn't even seen my girlfriends to cheer me up, but tonight was finally Starbucks night, and I couldn't wait!

Patty's birthday had been two weeks earlier, but we hadn't gone out for it yet. Normally, we would have celebrated ASAP, but this year she'd been evasive about getting together on the weekends, which was unusual for her. It *was* the big five-oh, which called for a large-scale celebration, so tonight we were going to make plans for the upcoming weekend. Kate thought we should go to New York City, which was only a half hour away. Barb and I were in agreement, but it was up to Patty to make the final decision. We also couldn't decide whether to do dinner and a play or dinner and dancing.

As we sipped our lattes and cappuccinos and tried to reach a verdict, I noticed that Patty's eyes had glazed over. *Hmm. What was that all about?* It was *her* birthday that we were discussing! She could act more interested!

"Earth to Patty." I waved my hands in front of her face. She actually blinked when she focused on me, so my suspicions were confirmed that she wasn't paying attention to us.

"That sounds like a good idea," she said.

"Really, Patty," Kate answered. "Exactly what idea would that be?" We stared at her and she started to look uncomfortable.

"Spill it, girl," demanded Barb. "You're holding out on us, and we want to know what you're not telling your best friends!"

"OK, OK," she relented. "I was going to tell you soon anyway, so it might as well be now." Barb, Kate, and I hunched forward, practically falling off our seats with anticipation. "Can you please sit back on your chairs? You look like three hungry cats about to pounce on one lone mouse!" I looked at Kate and Barb. Patty was right. We did look overeager and maybe a little crazed too, so we moved ourselves to a more relaxed position, although the crazed looks remained. I thought perhaps we were gossip-deprived since nothing juicy had been going on in our lives since my hot flash hospitalization incident.

Patty took a deep breath and said, "I met a guy, and we've been dating for a month. I didn't want to say anything until we had gone out a few times, in case it didn't work out. I always tell you about the men in my life right away and then it doesn't work out, and I feel foolish. I mean...you're married, and I'm still trying to find Mr. Right. Sometimes it's embarrassing."

Kate, with her usual candor, yelled so loud that everyone in the café could hear her, "What's his name? Is he cute? Where did you meet him? What does he do for a living? Where does he live? How old is he?" I shushed Kate and glanced around us. Sure enough, everyone was staring in our direction. The kids who were working tonight looked over with interest too.

Patty did have a point regarding always telling us too soon about her new flames. For such a pretty and intelligent woman, she had absolutely the worst taste in men. It had been like this since we were in high school. The truth was that she was drawn to losers. Most of the time, these men were decent-to-good-looking, but they would turn out to be poor (and looking for a woman to take care of them) or married (and looking for a fling) or crazy (and looking for someone to stalk). They always turned out to possess some undesirable quality that caused Patty to end the relationship. I shuddered to think what was wrong with this new guy, but I didn't say a word.

"Kate! Relax," Patty said. "I'll tell you all about him,

but first I was wondering if you three wouldn't mind doing a couples' night for my birthday instead of only the
four of us. I thought that it would be a more comfortable
scenario for him if your husbands were present."

"Why don't I host the get-together next Saturday?" I
said. "I can do hors d'oeuvres all night to keep the setting
casual. A sit-down dinner might be too formal for the
first meeting. What do you think, Patty?"

"Jill! You're the best and that sounds perfect! This
way, the guys can mingle and we can watch from afar, so
to speak. It will give me an opportunity to study how
Dave interacts with people other than me."

With those words, Kate was on her feet. "Dave! His
name is Dave! I like that name!"

Patty laughed and looked relieved that she had finally told us about her boyfriend. "I'll tell you the basics
now, but I'd like you to form your own opinions when
you meet him," she began. "His name is Dave LaRosa,
and he owns LaRosa's Artsy Flowers in Manhattan. He's
fifty-two years old, never married and no kids. He thinks
that marriage and children go hand in hand, so since he
never wanted children, he chose not to get married either.
He's had two serious relationships, but the women inevitably wanted to get married, so the relationships ended."
She paused.

"Well," piped up Barb, "I'm not so sure about this
no-marriage attitude. I thought that you wanted to get
married. What if you get serious and want to, but he
doesn't, and that's that? You'll just get hurt!"

"Listen, girls, since I know you're all thinking the
same thing as Barb: I need to start being realistic. I don't

even know anymore if I actually *do* want to get married. I've become very accustomed to my single life and the privacy it affords me. I'm set in my ways, and I don't have to answer to anyone. I'm certainly past my childbearing years, so all in all, is marriage really that important? I'm going to keep an open mind with Dave and see how it goes."

"What does he look like?" cried an exasperated Kate for the second time. "You're dating him for a month and regaling us with his marital philosophies. I know you, Patty! Any minute now, you're going to be whipping his résumé out of your everything-but-the-kitchen-sink pocketbook! I want the fun details, like did you have sex yet? Is he, you know, well-endowed?"

I looked around the café. Yup. Everyone was officially staring and listening to us now.

After our laughter over Kate's usual upfront outburst, Patty concluded the Dave discussion and said, "He's six feet and lanky, I guess. His hair is blond, his eyes are blue, and no, Kate, I am *not* answering your last two questions, not yet anyhow. Those are all the questions I'm responding to tonight, so why don't we focus on next Saturday?" And that's what we did for the rest of the night.

As I drove home, I couldn't quell the uneasy feeling that dear Dave was somehow, someway, not going to be Patty's Mr. Right. I hoped I was wrong.

CHAPTER 11—MEET DAVE

"So, Jill? What do you think is going to be wrong with this guy Dave? You know there has to be something," said Vic as he carried the dining room chairs into the living room. Unless we were formally dining, our guests tended to gravitate toward the kitchen and living room to socialize. I knew that tonight the girls would most likely be in the kitchen and the guys in the living room because there was a Mets game on television. Vic and Lou were huge fans and tried not to miss the nighttime or weekend games. One birthday about ten years ago, I'd bought my husband a very small portable television so he could watch the Mets and the Jets when we were at Neil's baseball or soccer games. While Neil ran up and down the soccer field, Vic would run up and down the sidelines with his TV in hand.

"I'm trying to be optimistic," I answered, "but it's difficult with her track record. Let's just say that I'm keeping my expectations at an all-time low. Maybe this time Patty will surprise me, but I'm not very hopeful. Wow! I can't believe I just said that! What a crappy friend I am!"

"Well, you'd better plaster that big smile of yours on because someone's here, and they're a half hour early, too," complained Vic. He hated it when people showed up too early or too late.

Kate and Lou walked in, accompanied by Barb and her husband, Jerry. Lou and Jerry seemed to be deep in stock market talk already. Jerry lived and breathed Wall Street, sometimes to the point of boredom, but he's Barb's husband, not mine, so I tried to overlook it. They'd been married for twenty-three years, and I truly believed that the only reason they were still together was because of his overlong work hours. He was a nice enough guy and a good husband, but he was also downright dull. Lou, on the other hand, was a lot like Vic with similar interests, which was probably why they got along so well. Both were fun-loving, sports-oriented guys. They were also hardworking people, but they didn't allow their jobs to rule their lives. The three men golfed together, sometimes going away for a few days on trips, and Vic said that Jerry lightened up on the broker talk during those times, but that was only because he redirected his obsessiveness to his golf game.

I pulled Kate and Barb into the kitchen and said, "You know how unnerved Vic gets about early arrivals.

Now he's going to be off his game the whole evening! *Ugh!* I need him focused so he can assess Dave! You two had better go put him back in a good mood! Or else..." I think I scared them, because they scurried over to Vic and started asking him golf questions. Talking golf was the one thing that could always cheer my husband up, and if that didn't work, compliments on his home craftsman-ship were a good fallback.

A short time later, the doorbell rang, announcing the arrival of the guests of honor. Poor Dave. We were not a reserved group of people. As soon as Patty and Dave walked into the living room, all talking ceased and six pairs of eyes turned to observe the new guest. Barb and Kate quickly composed themselves and walked over to greet them with kisses and hugs.

I held back for a minute to give Dave a onceover while he was otherwise occupied with everyone else. He was exactly as Patty had described him. With his light hair and eyes, he could be Patty's brother, with the excep-tion of the fact that he towered over her. Although he was casually dressed in expensive jeans, an equally pricy but-ton-down shirt, and what looked to be a pair of two-hundred-dollar sneakers, he gave the appearance of being dressed up. I didn't know if it was the way he carried himself with his perfect posture or the way his clothes were perfectly pressed or that his mid-length hair had not moved during the kisses and handshakes.

"You must be our delightful host, Jill," he said as he walked over and gave me a cool kiss on the cheek. "I've heard so much about you that I feel as if I know you, ac-tually all of you, already." He handed me a basket of artfully arranged sunflowers (my favorite flower), orange gerbera daisies, and red lilies. For a second, I had this strange, brief image of Dave skipping through a field picking the most perfect flowers to fill his basket. I shook my head. Now where had *that* image come from? I thanked him for his beautiful gift and placed the basket in the center of the kitchen table. Next to it, I placed the fine bottle of red wine that he had given to Vic. Well, he had good taste in wine and attention to detail with flowers. Then again, he *was* a florist! I glanced at him and felt that he had chosen the perfect occupation for himself.

As anticipated, the women stayed mostly in the kitchen to chat while the men set up camp in front of the TV, rising occasionally to refill a drink or a plate. I heard Dave confess that he was not much of a sports fan. He claimed that his business kept him very busy, leaving little time to devote to sports viewing. Instead of seeing this as a negative virtue, Vic and Lou seized the opportunity to create a baseball fan, and not just any old baseball follower, but a true-blue Mets fan! I studied Dave's expressions, and although he appeared to be following the sports talk, I had the distinct impression that beneath his smiling facade, he was totally uninterested.

"Well, what do you think of Dave?" asked Patty. "Isn't he a cutie? He made that basket himself, Jill, and filled it with your favorite flowers! He's so thoughtful!" My friend beamed with happiness. I knew that bringing him here to meet us was a big move for her. I could tell that she really liked him a lot, but I wasn't ready to drop my trepidations just yet. I was not going to base my opinion on one meeting with him—and my first, no less. People were always initially on their best behavior, so first impressions were not necessarily the most accurate.

Kate, naturally, was ready to voice her opinion. "He's good-looking. He seems nice, although it's a little hard to tell since Lou and Vic are doing all of the talking. They're probably boring the poor guy to death. I do have to say, though, that I've never seen such perfectly pressed clothes on a guy! Maybe it's a florist thing. Have you guys had sex yet?" Yup, that was Kate always getting straight to the point!

"Kate! You're relentless," whispered Patty. "I'm going to answer you just so you leave me alone. The answer is no, we have not had sex yet! If it will shut you up, you'll be the first I call when we do."

"Go easy on her, Patty," said Barb. "You know how she loves dirt and details. And by the way, why haven't you guys done the dirty deed yet? I hope he's not saving himself for marriage, because then you're out of luck!" With that exclamation and a couple of glasses of wine already consumed by each of us, silliness set in. Barb, Kate, and I were rolling on the floor laughing as Patty started snorting! "Hey, girl! Does he know that you snort? If not, he does now." We quickly looked into the living room, and sure enough, Dave was staring at Patty with his mouth agape. His expression caused us to erupt in even louder gales of laughter. The one thing about the four of us was that once we drank and got goofy, there was no turning back!

Oliver jumped up on Patty and barked at her strange noises, so the kitchen became very noisy. Lou and Vic yelled at us to keep it down. (Heaven forbid that they not be able to hear the game.) Jerry seemed to have disappeared, and I would have hazarded a guess that he was outside on a work-related phone call.

"Wow! You're a loud bunch, aren't you?" said Dave from the doorway. "And Patty? Was that unappealing noise coming from *you*?"

Poor Patty. She looked taken aback by his remark, but I jumped in quick with the save. "Oh, no, Dave. That was Oliver. He makes those sounds when he gets excited." Since Oliver was sitting on Patty's lap, the excuse was plausible. The only problem was that as Dave took a few steps closer to us, Oliver barked at him. He did this in a playful manner, but Dave didn't know that, and he quickly stepped away, appearing to be afraid of the dog. Again, I piped up: "Don't worry. He never bites. He just barks to get your attention and to get you to play with him."

"Sorry, but I'm not a dog person," confessed Dave. "Actually, I'm not really an animal lover. I suppose that I'm more of a people person. It's probably a result of my business interactions, you know? It's not as if I have any dog or cat customers! Ha-ha!"

Dave's "ha-ha!" brought our "ha-has" to an abrupt end. Now I had been forced by Dave to take his dislike of animals into my formation of an opinion of him. I knew that I wasn't being fair, but, unlike Dave, I was a huge animal lover, so I didn't take kindly to those who weren't. Kate and Barb started conversing quietly, and Patty announced that she was going outside to show her boyfriend our new deck. I thought that she really wanted to get him away from me quickly before I turned into my animal advocate self. I watched them leave and laughed because, unbeknownst to Dave, Oliver was right on their heels. He would never miss an opportunity to go out and chase squirrels. Sure enough, barking loudly, my dog was off in a flash across the yard, startling poor Dave, who nearly climbed a nearby tree in his haste to flee. I saw Patty patting his arm in feigned sympathy as she forced him to take a seat on one of the built-in benches on the deck.

"What a wimp," remarked Vic, who had arrived in the kitchen just in time to see Dave's overreaction. "What's with that guy? Can you believe that he doesn't like baseball?" I thought about the simplicity of how guys judged other guys; if you didn't like sports or were afraid of a small, harmless dog, then you were deemed unmanly and not friend material.

Women are much more complicated in their judgments, I thought as I set out a variety of desserts and started the coffee pot brewing. *We look at the face, the body, the sense of humor, and the intelligence level, and then we narrow those traits down even further. We are tough critics, but when we choose our mate, he usually has passed a stringent qualities test.*

Apparently either the Mets were sorely losing or the game was over, because the television was currently off, so all of us settled down in the living room for coffee and dessert. There was a chocolate mousse cake garnished with chocolate syrup and cherries, a variety of Italian pastries, and a bowl of strawberries and blueberries with whipped cream on the side. I didn't know whose eyes got bigger at the delectable treats, Kate's or Oliver's, but both looked ready to pounce!

Dave appeared to have calmed down. Jerry was off the phone for the moment. Lou and Vic had concluded their sports talk. Now was the time for a conversation that all eight of us could participate in. Patty said that for her birthday, Dave had taken her to see *Jersey Boys*, which was our favorite play. We had all seen it together two years ago and wanted to go back and see it again, but scheduling conflicts had kept this from happening. We chatted about plays for a while, which led to a discussion on the pros of living in a metropolitan area. Dave was the only one of us who lived in New York City, and he became a bit overzealous in extolling the benefits of his residence choice. As a matter of fact, after a while he seemed to be the only one speaking, as apparently the benefits were endless.

The sound came loud and clear; Kate, who had fallen asleep while Dave was talking, not only started snoring but also looked to be on the verge of falling off her chair. She tilted precariously to the right, and as I jumped up to grab her, I accidentally kicked Oliver, who had fallen asleep by my feet. Oliver, sensing that something fun was happening, barked, which successfully brought Dave's speech to an end. I guessed that must have been Dave's cue to depart because he stood up, towing Patty with him. Oliver hated it when people had to leave. He ran over and jumped up and down on Dave's legs, causing the poor guy to lose his balance and topple back onto the couch. My dog seized the opportunity to further show Dave his love and affection by jumping on the back of the couch and kissing Dave's face and biting his ear. Dave waved his hand as if he was swatting a fly or ready to faint or maybe both, judging by the look on his face.

Kate had woken up in the commotion, and Vic was finally able to grab the dog, ending his loving assault on our non-animal-lover guest. Dave grabbed Patty by the hand, jumped up and away from the couch, and stated that it really was time for them to go as he had work tomorrow and still had to drive back to the city. He was as white as a ghost, and we all knew the real reason that he was exiting, but it *was* getting late and the party had to end sometime, so we thanked them for coming and bid them good-night. Barb and Jerry left right afterward, with Jerry once again deeply engrossed in another "important" phone call.

Lou shook Kate, who had fallen back asleep again sometime during the Oliver escapade. She opened her eyes, glanced around the now empty room, and said sleepily, "Well, that went well!"

CHAPTER 12—MY FAVORITE DAY OF THE YEAR

What were the chances that my son would be born on my favorite holiday, Halloween? I didn't have a clue, but much to my extreme happiness, he was! My due date was October 24, but apparently Neil wasn't ready to leave his warm, fluid-filled home yet. Really, who could blame him? For nine and a half months, he had been fed all manner of delicious foods from the time his mom woke up until the time she went to bed. If he was really lucky, she got up during the night and fed him some more! Where else could you get seven flavors of ice cream at one time, chips and Cheetos by the bagful, multiple candy bars at once, and every dessert set out on the table during holiday meals? Of course, there was good food too: a couple of steaks at a single sitting; baked potatoes with butter, sour cream, cheddar cheese, and bacon; entire roasted chickens; double bowls of pasta. The list went on and on as Mom gained thirty-eight pounds and Neil gained eight.

When it came time for Neil to make his grand entrance into the world, he fought it tooth and nail. The doctor, nurses, and Vic kept exclaiming, "I see the head! Keep pushing!" A couple of hours later, they were still saying the same things, but with less enthusiasm. They actually had the gall to look tired! Really? They were tired? I had a big round pumpkin (it *was* Halloween) stuck in my you-know-whatsits, and *they* were tired! Anyway, my son got to keep that perfect round head of his, because he arrived via caesarean section at 5:50 p.m., and I swear that when he looked at me with his beautiful gray eyes, he asked, "What's for dinner?"

"What's for dinner, Mom?" *Cripes!* I jumped sky-high as Neil's voice startled me out of my musings. He and Vic had this habit of sneaking up on me when I was lost in thought (which was quite often) and scaring the bejesus out of me. They swore that they didn't do it on purpose, but I suspected otherwise. In truth, Neil really didn't do it often, but Vic, who was six feet tall and 185 pounds, walked like a ballerina. That's OK. One of these days, I'll drop dead from a Vic-induced heart attack, and my dear husband will have to live with the constant guilt, after, of course, he pays off the house and buys a new car for himself and Neil.

"Where do you want to go for your eighteenth birthday? Someplace special?" I asked him after my heart slowed to a reasonable rate. His birthday was tomorrow, but we were going to celebrate tonight with Gabby, Pete, and Jason. Tomorrow was Halloween, and I needed to be home to distribute the ten bags of candy I'd purchased in anticipation of hordes of trick-or-treaters, plus Neil had to be back at college on Sunday.

My son named his favorite place to eat, which, as luck would have it, was my least favorite place. "Can't we go somewhere else?" I implored. "A restaurant with edible food, perhaps?" I knew he wouldn't change his mind, but I had to give it a shot.

"No," he answered. "That's where I want to go. Anyway, you said that I could pick the place, so I'm picking it."

Oh well. He is right, and I really shouldn't complain. Neil's an easy-going, undemanding kid. He hadn't even asked for any birthday gifts, although I still had purchased him a few presents that I knew he would like. At least my sister-in-law was going, so she and I could drink lots of celebratory wine and grumble to each other about the food.

Besides my best friends, Gabby was one of my favorite people in the world. Our husbands were not just brothers; they also were each other's closest friends. Ever since Gabby came into the family picture, the four of us had spent a lot of time together, sometimes simply going out for dinner or day trips, and almost always taking summer vacations together. When our sons were born just three weeks apart, they naturally fell into the already established family closeness. I thought back again to my pregnancy. How ironic that Gabby and I had conceived within weeks of each other, thus enabling us to share in the joys of pregnancy and subsequent motherhood. It was an experience that had forged our bond forever, and as we got older, it truly seemed that we did become closer and closer.

Neil's eighteenth birthday had me feeling a tad sentimental. I looked at my son and thought how handsome he was. When he smiled, his face lit up and his eyes sparkled. Personally, I thought he looked like my dad and brother, but I'm sure that Vic thought he looked like him. One thing was for certain: they talked and walked exactly the same. If I called the house, I didn't know which one was answering the phone, although that was probably because I had gone into shock that someone had *actually* answered the phone. Frequently I was stuck walking behind them since heaven forbid they should slow down to my pace! I was able to view their father-and-son shoulders-hunched-with-feet-out waddle. If I didn't look at their heads, I couldn't tell who was who. Back in my grammar school days, I would have shot rubber bands at them. I could just envision the two of them feeling the back of their heads to see what was causing the stinging sensation. As the vision clearly formed in my very imaginative mind, I laughed out loud.

"Mom! Are you telling yourself jokes again? You look like a nut, standing there laughing at nothing!" Neil quickly exited the room as if we were in a roomful of people and I had embarrassed him. I was used to it though, and I just laughed harder. According to my son, I was the most embarrassing mother on earth. I could tell him a thing or two about parental humiliation! He should have grown up with my kerchief-clad, polyester-encased mother.

"Hell-oooo! Anyone home?" came my father-in-law's voice from the foyer. "Your door was open, Jill. You need be more careful," he admonished as he walked into the kitchen with Mama.

"Papa, didn't you see Vic outside fixing the decorations?" I yelled since he was hard-of-hearing.

"I no see Victor," he answered looking a bit confused. "Is he here? Why you yell?"

"Never mind." I knew that they had probably walked from house to house through the mailman-created path between the homes. They still should have seen Vic, but they seemed to be oblivious to their surroundings when they were out and about. They also were absent-minded, and I had visions of them leaving their house and walking away, never to be seen again.

"¿Donde está mi niño?" inquired Mama. "I wish him happy birthday. You cook for him, Jill?" She looked toward my empty stove top, made a disapproving face, and said, "I cook for him."

I grabbed her arm as she opened my refrigerator door, "No, Ma. You're not cooking. We're going out for dinner."

"Ooh…you go out. Why you no cook? Pobre niño! Pedro! Give the card to Neil. We leave now. Jill no cook."

Papa hadn't heard her, as he had wandered into my laundry room and was inspecting the floor. I knew that he was looking for work to do. He had worked in construction all his life, and when he retired, Pete and Vic had frequently utilized his Mr. Fix-It skills, but no more. He was simply too old and would wind up creating more disaster where he was working. Even his once great painting skills had gone off the wall (literally). Now he mostly tried to help his sons by peering over their shoulders while they were working, then shining the light in their eyes instead of on the object to be fixed. I frequently caught him standing outside his house and staring at it as if willing something to break so he could run and fix it. It drove me crazy, but I loved my father-in-law, so I'd stand and watch him to make sure that he didn't wander off. If I spotted my mother-in-law out there, I'd find something to do on the opposite side of my house. Once in a while, I'd peek out to see if she was still there, and she always was. Oh well...wishful thinking...

"*Pedro!*" she yelled. "*Darle la tarjeta!*" Papa jumped up and rushed to Neil's room to give him his birthday card (no doubt stuffed with a few hundred-dollar bills) with Mama close behind.

As they were leaving, Mama once again threw me a dirty look, no doubt still miffed about the no-dinner situation. I heard Papa loudly exclaiming, "Victor! There you are! Where you were?" and then, "What you say?" followed by Vic's voice loudly responding to his dad. The neighbors were probably at their windows or on their porches catching their daily source of entertainment. Even I had to admit that my husband and his dad's conversations could become quite comical, especially when my father-in-law was having a particularly bad hard-of-hearing day.

Vic, Neil, and I left the house, and I stopped outside

to give the Halloween decorations a final inspection. There were bats and spiders hanging from our Japanese maple tree along with large moaning mummies. The walkway was lined with light-up pumpkins that grinned and blinked as you passed. But the pièce de résistance was the spiderweb-enclosed graveyard at the base of the maple. Everywhere were tombstones interspersed with body parts either sticking out of the ground or randomly lying around. Tomorrow I would put out the last item, a fog and sound machine that would be sure to shock and entertain the trick-or-treaters.

"Jill! Are you coming? The decorations are done, so do *not* think that I'm going to change anything that you've now decided doesn't look right," Vic announced with exasperation.

I walked to the car, and as I caught a glimpse of his face, I experienced my own Halloween shock. Vic was giving me the same dirty look that his mother had given me earlier! *Oh no! I married my mother-in-law*, I thought with alarm. *Look at him! He's giving me the evil eye!* Sadly, this was not the first time I'd had that thought. The older he got, the more Vic looked like her. He also had certain mannerisms that were just like hers, like the way he held his head or pursed his lips when he was angry or the way that he became neurotically obsessed with his aches and pains. It was downright creepy.

I heard Neil grumbling from the backseat, but I ignored him. The two of them despised the holiday seasons, beginning with Halloween—or, more accurately, they despised *me* during the holidays because I made them work. I liked the outside of my house to be lavishly decorated. I mean, it was only twice a year, right? Halloween and Christmas. You would think that I was torturing them, the way they complained about something that took a total of a day to complete (and not even a full day, at that).

I missed my son's younger years, when he would happily help with the decorations. He actually *wanted* to be of assistance, and we would be outside for hours until everything was completed perfectly. He would let me create awesome Halloween costumes, and we would go out trick-or-treating for hours. I had as much fun as he did! Somewhere along the years, he decided that mom-created costumes were undesirable, and even more to my dismay, he wanted to trick-or-treat with his friends! I was crushed! Now I had to wait for grandkids. I knew that even if I was old and feeble, I was going to be pounding that pavement once again.

"Hey, Mom! Do you want me to give out the candy tomorrow before I have to head back to school?" I smiled at my son's question as I nodded. He might be eighteen, and yes, he really didn't like to decorate any longer, but he still loved the holiday as much as I did. He laughed as he recounted the unforgettable Oliver Halloween story. "Do you remember when Oliver was a puppy and he stole the Butterfinger from the candy bowl? You were scream-ing and running down the block with him in your arms, terrified he was going to choke! But he didn't, Mom. Remember the next day when he pooped out the wrapper minus the candy that was inside? How funny was that?"

Neil, Vic, and I were laughing hard as we pulled into the restaurant parking lot, where Pete, Gabby, and Jason awaited. Despite the terrible fare (in Gabby's and my opinions), we all had our usual great time! My baby was eighteen!

CHAPTER 13—CASTILLO HOLIDAYS

"We should go away for the holidays. What do you think, Jill?" asked my husband as he pulled out box after box after box of Christmas decorations. It was the Friday after Thanksgiving. While the rest of the country were trudging through stores and malls in search of the biggest and hottest Black Friday deals, the Castillo family was home preparing to decorate for the holiday season, and the men were not happy.

I know the holidays are supposed to be a time of peace, love, and happiness, and I swear that I used to believe that, but not anymore. There seemed to be too many mandatory, time-consuming, holiday-related chores. I'd been doing them for twenty-four years, and I thought I was suffering from "the most wonderful time of the year" burnout.

Every year, I shopped at the beginning of November in the hope that I would be finished by the beginning of December. Well, that never happened. There were always those last-minute or hard-to-find gifts that took more time to shop for than all of the other gifts on the list combined. For example, there was the year that Neil and every other kid in the world wanted the Xbox 360 game system. I spent hours every single day searching online for it until I found it on December 23, then had to pay an extra shipping fee to have it delivered the next day. I had to admit, though, that it was worth it just to see his eyes light up and a grin spread from ear to ear when he opened the much-anticipated present.

Then there were always those friends and family members who "don't want anything." I mean, seriously, there's not a single item that a person needs or wants? I know if I actually don't give those individuals a gift, they're going to hold it against me for the rest of my life. So I traipse through the stores in search of that "perfect" gift. Of course I never find it, so I wind up purchasing any old thing because I've reached the point where I really don't care anymore.

All of the gifts got stored in the attic. When it came time to wrap, I would find myself face to face with a daunting mountain of packages and then wonder why I'd been stupid enough to lug them up the two flights of stairs to the attic because now I had to carry them all back down again.

"Jill? Jill!" Vic looked at me oddly. "Why are you standing there crying?"

"Oh, I was just thinking about Christmas shopping," I replied, thinking to myself, *Something that you cannot relate to.* Again he looked at me strangely, but ceased his questions and resumed pulling out boxes. I think I unintentionally gave him a look, so I pretended that I was scrunching up my face while deep in thought.

Wow! There were a lot of boxes! Half of them were for the outside of the house and half for the inside. Was it always this many? *Ugh!* It was going to take me all weekend to get that stuff up. Next weekend we'd put up the tree, so there went that weekend too.

"Yes, let's go away," I said to Vic and I threw my arms around him. "Please!"

"First of all, I asked you that question fifteen minutes ago, and second, you know I was kidding, right?"

"Yeah. Yeah. But look at all of this stuff. I used to love decorating, and now I hate it!"

"Then don't do it. Or else stop complaining! Where do you want all of these boxes?" Vic gestured to the decoration-filled basement. "Can you ask Neil to come down and help please?"

I walked upstairs to where my son was playing the infamous Xbox, listening to music, watching TV, and playing Halo on the second TV set that he had brought home from school, all at *one* time! And they say men can't multitask. "Neil, can you please go help Dad with the boxes and decorations?"

"Today? We're doing them today? Now? I'm in the middle of a game. Can't he wait? I'll do them tomorrow."

I didn't answer him. There was no need. He knew that he'd better get his butt downstairs now, or his father was going to be in a fouler mood than he was already in. I stood in the doorway to his den and gave him the Mom stare. Neil and Oliver were intimidated by the Mom stare. Both of them tried to stare me down, but they never succeeded. Oliver usually slinked off whimpering, and I thought that Neil imagined doing the same thing. There were certain times when the Mom was not to be messed with, and now was one of those times, so he marched past me and down the stairs, grumbling something about "the benefits of living away from home." As far as I was concerned, if Vic and I could pay thousands of dollars a year for our son to get the education that he wanted while also residing at his chosen college, Neil could carry a few boxes for us in his off time! If Mama Castillo was here right now, she'd probably say that Neil was a "pobre niño!"

I was about to head back to the basement, but I heard a lot of grunting, muttering, and cursing from down there, so I hesitated at the top step and yelled, "Don't forget that next Friday is Hot Dog Friday." No answer. I yelled again, "Did you hear me?"

"We heard you!" screamed back a grumpy-sounding Neil, followed by more grunting and groaning sounds. No way was I going back downstairs again today! Actually, I should head to Starbucks for the rest of the day. Even Oliver was hiding under the coffee table. Smart dog! I'd do the same, but, as in the bathroom cabinet situation, I didn't think my rear end could squeeze under the table either.

I unpacked the inside decorations and thought about Hot Dog Friday. It was a tradition that Vic and I had unintentionally started during our first Christmas as husband and wife. Bent on finding the "perfect" Christmas tree, we had been shopping for hours one Friday night, with no satisfactory results. We realized that we were starving, so we stopped for hot dogs at a famous frankfurter establishment. The following year, while once again seeking that perfect fir or pine, we again stopped for hot dogs and a tradition was born. Sometimes it was the small, simple things that meant so much.

"Yikes!" I exclaimed, jolted out of my reverie. Speaking of small things, Oliver was running around crazily, tossing something in the air and then diving to attack and bark at it. "What do you have there, Oliver? Can Mommy see?" Always eager to please, Oliver ran up to me and tossed the item into my outstretched hands, then ran to the laundry room to be rewarded with the treat that he knew was kept there. I looked down and exclaimed, "Oh my! It's the baby Jesus! Oliver, you stole the baby Jesus!" Just as the words flew out of my mouth, Neil and Vic entered the living room, took one look at the slobbered-upon miniature newborn, and burst into laughter, putting an end to their irritable moods.

Baby Jesus had saved the day!

CHAPTER 14—DILEMMAS

Adiós, holidays, I happily thought as I packed up the last box of decorations and looked around at the endless array of cartons obscuring the kitchen floor. "Hooray! Another holiday bites the dust," I sang...my own version of Queen's "Another One Bites the Dust."

"*Mom!* Do you have to sing so loud? Better yet, do you have to sing at all?" yelled my son from two rooms away. What a party pooper he could be! It was January 2, a great day in my opinion because it was "Bye-Bye Decorations" day! Hopefully, when Vic got home, he and Neil would carry the boxes to their designated basement, closet, and crawl spaces, and once again all would be right with the world.

If I got lucky, I wouldn't have to lay my eyes on an-

other family member until Easter Sunday. I had been af-
flicted by family overload, but now I could breathe a sigh
of relief. I also missed my best friends, but at least I'd be
seeing them this week. Because of family obligations,
holiday girlfriend time was hard to come by, especially if
the four of us wanted to be together all at once.

So, four days later, I was contentedly settled in my
favorite Starbucks chair, surrounded by Patty, Kate, and
Barbara, and we rehashed our holiday ups and downs until we were officially caught up with one another's lives.

"I made a New Year's resolution," confessed Barbara. "I've decided that Jerry and I could use a little boost
to our marriage. I mean, I know he's a hard worker and
loves his job, but I don't think that we have enough 'us'
time. He's obsessed with work, and I'd like him to be obsessed with me sometimes. I can't remember the last time
we had sex!"

"I know what you mean," I responded. "Vic and I try
to make a point of doing the whole quality time thing,
especially with Neil away at college. My gripe with my
husband is that he doesn't notice me. It's a good thing
when I'm looking bad, but even when I'm looking good,
he doesn't say anything. A compliment once in a while
would be nice, don't you think?" Three heads nodded as-
sent as I continued. "Do you remember when my hair
was down to my waist and I cut six inches off of the back
and even more in the front for the face frame?" Again
three nods. "So I came home, and he and I were talking,
and I kept flipping my hair with my hand, waiting for
some type of comment. This must have gone on for about
ten minutes, until he finally asked me if there was some-

thing wrong with my hand!" Kate, Patty, and Barb guffawed as I pantomimed the hand/hair flipping action. "Anyway, Vic said that my hair didn't look any different. So I have to wonder, does he *really* look at me when he's looking at me? Because that was one very noticeable example that went unnoticed!"

"Don't complain," chastised Kate. "I have the opposite problem with Lou. He notices *everything*! He even tells me when I need to get a haircut! The other day he said that I looked like I was packing a few extra pounds around my middle. The nerve of him! Why do you think I'm wearing this loose, flowy top? At least it's in style, because it's really to disguise my new muffin-top that I'm now self-conscious about!"

"I wasn't finished!" yelled Barb, a little too loudly, as now all the Starbucks patrons were looking our way. "Sorry, people. Go back to your lattes." She continued on a quieter note. "So, I bought this *really* sexy pink-and-black bustier with matching lacy thong panties. I planned a super-romantic New Year's Eve: lobster dinner, oil-scented bath, candles everywhere, rose petals on the bed, and an unending supply of champagne. After our relaxing, romantic bath, I was going to put on my new outfit and wow him into hours of amazing sex. Do you know what it's like squeezing one of those teeny tiny thongs over this rear end? When I tried it on, it took me about ten minutes to untwist the sides. How do women regularly wear those things? Oh, and I forced him to mute his phone since I couldn't get him to turn it off. So the dinner was scrumptious, the champagne was bubbly and delicious, and the bath was warm and sensual. After that, he went to lie in bed and I wrestled into my sexy costume. It took me fifteen minutes this time to fix my boobs in their boob-enhancing cups, then to unscramble the wretched thong. Since I was oily and still a little wet, it was even harder, but when I was finished, even I had to admit that I looked great. My cheeks had a nice rosy flush to them." Kate giggled. "*I mean my face cheeks,* Kate! Anyway, I glided into the bedroom, all soft and warm and inviting, and *he's asleep!* First I got a little pissed, but then I realized I had taken too long to get ready, so I slid into bed with him and wrapped my arms and legs around him. And *he starts snoring!* Can you believe it?" The three of us rapidly shook our heads in disbelief and sympathy for our friend, and she continued, "He finally woke up, looked at me, and said, 'What took you so long? That bath made me so sleepy. Why don't we just cuddle?' And then he fell back asleep! I was so mad that I drank a bottle of champagne by myself and passed out in the guest bedroom, after I trashed those stupid thongs. And in conclusion, my dear friends, that was the beginning and the end of my New Year's resolution!" Barb stopped speaking.

For a minute, she looked like she was about to start crying, but then Kate said, "You wore a thong? I would have paid to see that! He should have had sex with you just as a reward for your courage. No way would I be caught dead in one of those things! And don't go getting any ideas now about burying me in a thong because I said that. I *will know,* and I'll haunt you three for all eternity!"

Kate's silly outburst succeeded in cheering Barb up, and apparently every other Starbucks customer, as I heard a lot of giggling behind me. Kate was the only person I knew who could garner laughter without even trying.

After the amusement died down and we replenished our drinks and completed a bathroom run, Barb asked, "So, Patty…now that the entire café knows about my sex life—or should I say "lack thereof"—why don't you tell them about yours, since you probably have the most exciting one out of all of us?"

Looking somewhat embarrassed, Patty replied quietly, "Well, we haven't really done it yet."

"You haven't had sex yet! What are you waiting for? Marriage?" exclaimed Kate, again much too loudly. She quickly looked around. "Oops! Sorry. Did it again, didn't I? I think I have self-control issues."

"At this point, maybe we should just invite everyone to come over and join us," said Patty. "They already know all of our business anyway." She sat quietly for a bit and sipped her cappuccino. "I don't really don't know what to say. There's been a lot of kissing and cuddling, but when I've tried to take it further, he stops me with some sort of excuse. He'll say he's tired or has a headache or he's just not in the mood."

"He sounds like a woman," piped up Kate again.

"He sounds like Jerry," laughed Barb, apparently greatly relieved to have the attention drawn away from her.

"Honestly, you guys, I really, really like him, but I'm horny as hell! Frustrated, too!" Patty added, "If this keeps up, I may be able to claim virginity status again. It's probably growing back as I speak. Seriously, any suggestions?"

"I'll lend you my bustier and thong," volunteered Barb. "Sorry, I meant just the bustier. I forgot I threw out the thong. Plus, after my disaster, I'm probably not the best one to give advice."

"Don't look at me," Kate said, waving her hands in front of her. "I've been so hormonal lately, Lou is afraid to come near me. I feel like I'm bipolar with the extreme mood swings. I can't sleep at night with those hot flashes! All I do is get up to change my pajamas. One minute I'm cold, and the next, I'm hot as hell! And to top it all off, I think I'm drying up like a prune down there, if you know what I mean! Yuck!"

"Hey! I'm going to be married twenty-five years soon! My seduction techniques deserted me about the time Neil was born. This menopause thing has me so forgetful, I'm lucky if I even remember how to have sex," I reported, then continued. "Maybe he has something really special planned for you. Are you two going away anytime soon?"

"No place that I'm aware of," answered Patty. "But you're right, Jill. Maybe he wants to wait for a special, perfect moment. I should stop complaining. He's a nice guy and we have fun together. I'm sure the intimate stuff will come with time. Right? Unless he doesn't like sex— then I don't know what to do. I'd say I'm screwed, but unfortunately that's not the case!"

We laughed uneasily. It really wasn't funny though, and I knew Barb and Kate felt as bad for Patty as I did. I was beginning to think Dave was going to turn out to be one more loser on Patty's long list of losers, and I didn't know how many more bad romances she could handle.

As if reading my thoughts, Patty dejectedly declared, "If this relationship doesn't work out, I'm giving up men forever! I may even consider becoming a lesbian!"

I swore that I heard some of our fellow patrons gasp and fall off of their chairs at that comment! After tonight, we might have to find a new Starbucks to frequent!

CHAPTER 15—JILL GETS A JOB

With Neil away at college and not in need of my constant
care and attention, I decided I wanted to do something for
myself, specifically something that would allow me to
earn money of my own. Giving up my career as a proba-
tion officer to bring up my son had been worth it. I would
never have wanted to miss out on all the rewarding experiences of raising him, but the one downside had been my
forced dependency on Vic for my monetary needs.

Over the last eighteen years, I'd made a few attempts
at returning to the job force, but for one reason or another, they didn't work out. What I basically wanted was
something that I could do part-time, on my schedule, with
me as my own boss. The idea of answering to another
person for minimum wage did not appeal to me in the

least. Apparently, when your résumé read that your most recent jobs have been those of "mom," "homemaker," and "husband's personal assistant," you were not in high demand. Unless, of course, some other parent was looking for a "mom/homemaker/personal assistant." I once met a female attorney who hired a person to handle childcare and all the household responsibilities. When she was describing her employee, she said to me, "I hired myself a wife, and it's great! I don't have to worry about a thing at home. I get to go to work and then come home, relax, and spend quality time with my kids. I feel like a man!"

Wow! I was so envious of that woman. I went home that night and asked Vic if I could get a wife, and he said, "No."

After careful consideration of my options, which were not plentiful, I came up with what I thought was a brilliant idea. I was going to utilize my personal assistant and chauffeuring skills; I was going to develop a business. For a fee, I would drive elderly people to their daily destinations, whether it was for food shopping or appointments. If they needed me, I'd also aid them while they were at these places.

I created colorful flyers to distribute around my town and also hang up at the community center. These flyers had pictures of happy seniors being escorted from their homes to their destinations by an equally happy me.

"What's with the pictures of old people?" came Vic's voice from behind me. Startled, I gave a little yelp, spilling my coffee on poor Oliver, who had been sleeping at my feet. At least the coffee was cold, but Oliver now looked like a jumping, barking Milk Dud. I grabbed him quickly before he could scatter coffee stains all over the house, and started wiping the liquid off with a wet towel. "Sorry," said Vic meekly, "but didn't you hear me come in?"

"I never hear you come in because you purposely sneak in and up to me on purpose! Can't you just walk like a normal person once in a while, instead of like Casper the Friendly Ghost Husband? Seriously, Vic! You're too big to walk so softly! Did you take ballet lessons as a kid?" As I yelled at my light-footed spouse, I vigorously toweled Oliver until I noticed that he was cowering. My dog hated it when people yelled or acted angry. It went too much against his "I'm so happy and I love everyone" disposition, and he just couldn't handle it psychological-ly. I forced myself to calm down. At least the coffee hadn't spilled on my freshly printed flyers.

"For your information," I told Vic, "I'm going to ad-vertise myself as a senior citizen driver. I'm sure there are a lot of elderly people in or around our town who could use someone to provide transportation for a fee. I want to earn a little spending money so I don't always have to answer to you regarding my expenditures. It will give me a little monetary freedom, something I haven't had in years."

"Whatever makes you happy, although I doubt you're going to find customers easily," replied my "glass is half-empty" husband. I could tell that he had already lost interest in my little business venture anyway. As far as he was concerned, as long as my ideas did not greatly affect or change his life, he was fine with them. I really wished he could be more positive about my ambition.

"What makes me happy is shoes and lots of them!" I yelled at his receding back, just to annoy him in retaliation for his lack of enthusiasm. *Ah, shoes!* They were my greatest addiction: flats, low heels, high heels, thongs, boots, ballet-style, mules, sandals—the list went on and on. And so many colors to choose from that sometimes I felt the need to buy a fantastic shoe in every available color. So what if I only wore a pair a few times? It was all about the joy I felt upon sliding those beautiful new shoes onto my happily waiting feet and wiggling, anticipatory toes.

"You're still thinking about shoes, aren't you?" asked Vic as he headed to the basement to exercise. "I can tell by that look of pleasure on your face. I'm sure you probably need some more pairs too. The hundred or so that you own aren't enough, are they?"

I could have argued with him on the subject, but why waste my time? We would never, ever agree on my shoe obsession and the fact that they were necessary for my contented existence. I had tried many times to explain to my obtuse husband that shoes, for women, were like sex for men. You simply could never have enough.

"Wow! Did I digress! I need to get back to work now," I said. I frequently spoke my thoughts out loud when I was alone. It wasn't a big deal, except that I had taken to doing it so often, I sometimes found myself also talking to myself when I was out and about. After a few episodes of people peering at me strangely, I started to wear my Bluetooth earpiece when I was not at home, so it appeared as if I were on my cell phone.

The next day I posted my flyers at some local businesses, the public library and the senior citizens' community center. Within two weeks, I had received several phone calls. It already seemed that this new business of mine was going to be interesting and comical.

My first call was from Mr. Smith, who wanted to know if I cleaned toilets. I very nicely informed Mr. Smith that I gagged when I cleaned my own toilet, so no, I would not be willing to clean his. I don't think that he was pleased with my response, as he informed me that if I wasn't able to clean bowls, then I probably wasn't good at anything.

OK, that went well, I thought as I hung up with the non-endearing senior.

My next phone call was from Mrs. Robinson. I swear that was her real name, and all I could envision throughout the call was an elderly "cougar" with a younger, forty-something-year-old boyfriend already taking care of her "needs." Mrs. Robinson wanted to know if I provided lawn care and shoveling services, to which I once again had to reply no. Wow! I didn't even do that at my own house.

Unfortunately, there were other phone calls from seniors requiring services that I was not providing. It really made me wonder if these folks actually *read* the information on my flyers!

Gertrude and Ed Noodle were my next callers, and they sounded exactly like the type of clients I was seeking. I spoke with Gertrude, who informed me that her husband was partially blind and more than partially deaf, so their children had insisted that he relinquish his car. Gertrude had apparently never learned to drive, so they needed someone to chauffer them around a couple of times a week. Mr. and Mrs. Noodle's children were busy with jobs and their own children, so Gertrude did not want to impose on them. She thought my service sounded perfect for her needs. We arranged to meet the following day at the public library.

On the morning of my meeting with the Noodles, I received a call from Mrs. Matilda Funnier, who right off the bat sternly informed me that her name was pronounced "Foon-ier," and to please not call her "Funnier," as she did not like it when people mispronounced her surname. She also stated, in a no-nonsense tone, that I should refer to her as "Mrs. Funnier" and not "Matilda." Yikes! This one was going to be a tough old cookie, but then again, could I really be choosy when beginning my business? I had two clients to start off with, which was exactly what I had wanted. I took a deep breath and inquired when Mrs. Funnier would like to meet with me, and we decided on this evening, also at the public library.

A short time later, dressed in black pants and a black turtleneck, with a bright green scarf to brighten both my eyes and the outfit, I set out to meet the Noodles.

They were already there and waiting patiently when I arrived. Gertrude stood straight and tall at about five feet six inches. Ed was shorter and looked to be about my height. Both were of medium build. Gertrude had a full head of blue-white hair, and Ed was bald. They had kindly blue eyes, but Ed's had a twinkle to them, which led me to believe that he probably had a good sense of humor.

I approached them and put out my hand, saying,

"Hello, Mr. and Mrs. Noodle. I'm Jill."

I assumed that Mrs. Noodle took an immediate liking to me because she ignored my outstretched hand and proceeded to give me a hug. "I just knew who you were as soon as I set eyes on you! You remind me of our daughter, Sara! Doesn't she, Ed? Ed? *Ed!*"

A startled Mr. Noodle jumped six inches off the ground as if someone had goosed him, and I clenched my teeth to refrain from laughing in the poor man's face. He recovered himself quickly, though, and shook hands with me. I guessed that the male Noodle was not the spontaneous hugger that his wife was. He did give me a quick wink as if we had shared a private joke, although I wasn't quite sure exactly what the joke was. What the heck! I winked back anyway. Hopefully he hadn't been flirting, or I was really going to be in trouble with the missus.

"Why don't we take a seat in the library and talk so we can get to know each other a little?" I suggested. We sat at a table, and Gertrude took a piece of paper out of her pocketbook and spread it before her. She then fumbled again in her bag. This went on for five minutes while Ed sat there staring at the bookshelves and shaking his head.

"Mrs. Noodle? Did you lose something?" I asked. Her face was gradually taking on a flustered appearance. Mr. Noodle snickered, which earned him a scowl from his spouse.

She finally looked up at me. "Lordy! I do believe I left my reading glasses at home! However will I read my questions and write your answers? Oh my!"

Ed laughed and managed to spit out, "Gertie, dear!

They're on top of your head, just like they always are! Why do you leave them there if you're never going to remember them?"

Gertrude patted the crown of her head and exclaimed, "Oh! There they are! Ed, you know I put them there so I don't lose them. And please stop laughing at me."

"Well, you may not lose them, but you always forget where they are. Can't you find a better place?" replied the still smiling Ed.

As much as I was getting a kick out of their exchange, I needed to put an end to it, as both were speaking loudly and the other library patrons were glaring and shushing us. Between Mrs. Noodle talking noisily because of her husband's lack of hearing and Mr. Noodle yelling so he could hear himself, we sounded like we were having a party at our table.

I needed to get this meeting over and done with before the stern-faced head librarian kicked us out.

Instead of letting Gertrude read her questions aloud to me, I read the inquiries myself in a much quieter tone of voice, then answered them and wrote down my responses for her benefit. After about an hour of discussion, the Noodles agreed that they wanted to hire me. Basically, they needed my services for food shopping, occasional bank visits, and doctors' appointments. We established that Mondays would be grocery days. The bank and doctors would be on an as-needed basis, and would probably have to be worked into a schedule that included my (anticipated) other client.

That evening, I returned to the library to meet Mrs.

Funnier, who in appearance was the opposite of Mrs. Noodle. Matilda Funnier was short and stocky like a fire hydrant. She had dyed-brown hair and no twinkle to her alert and assessing brown eyes. The whole conversation took about fifteen minutes. In a clipped voice, she asked me a few questions about myself, including whether I'd ever been arrested. For a brief second, I had the impulse to make up a story about a conviction for scamming old people, but I somehow didn't think that Mrs. Funnier would think it was funny, so I held my tongue. After all, I needed to be a mature businesswoman right now.

She stood up to indicate that our discussion was concluded and said, "Well, I suppose you'll do. I prefer to food-shop on Wednesdays, and I always go to the bank on Fridays to check my balance. Afternoons are for naps and cooking, so we'll conduct our business in the morning, unless, of course, I have a medical appointment later in the day. I believe that about covers it, so I will see you next Wednesday at 10 a.m." As she turned to exit the library, she added, "Oh, and one more thing. I will need you to go grocery shopping with me and carry my bags. Good evening, Jill." And with that, she left. I realized as I watched her that she had never removed her hat and coat while she was here. I had an uneasy feeling that Mrs. Funnier was not going to be a joy to work for.

I walked home with a little skip to my step. This whole chauffeuring idea might or might not work out, but I felt optimistic. I mean…I was only going to be driving seniors around. How bad could it be?

CHAPTER 16—WHO'S DAVE?

Patty called an emergency assembly of The Forever 39ers on Sunday afternoon at our usual meeting place. Kate and Barb were already there, joking with the baristas, when I arrived. I ordered my caramel macchiato, and we sat down on the corner seats to wait for Patty. The huge windows provided a bird's-eye view of the parking lot, so we'd know as soon as she arrived.

"I feel like something's wrong," I said to my friends. "First she calls a meeting out of the blue on an unscheduled day, and then she's late. Patty is *never* late! It's Sunday, so we know it's not a traffic issue."

"I have a bad feeling about this," answered Barb. "Do you think she's sick?"

"I don't think so," Kate joined in. "I spoke with her a

few days ago, and she sounded fine, although I did detect a distracted tone to her voice, but I just wrote it off as her being busy. I figured she was probably reorganizing her handbag or something while we were on the phone."

"I wish she could organize my brain," I said. "My memory is becoming so bad that I have to leave Post-Its to remind me where the other Post-Its are! One of these days, you're going to see a picture of me in the local paper: 'Wandering Woman Found with Post-It on Her Forehead. Please Claim Her!'"

In the midst of our laughter over that image, Patty walked in and we all stopped in mid-laugh. Not only was she fifteen minutes late (which doesn't sound like much, but to Patty, even five minutes late was unacceptable), but she also had no make-up on, she was still wearing pajama bottoms, and her hair was sticking out in all directions. This was definitely not the hair of the woman who had looked like a shampoo model at my birthday party. Who was this person, and what had she done with our Patty?

Leave it to tactful Kate to exclaim, "Oh my! What happened to your hair?"

Barb gave Kate a "shut your big mouth" look, and said, "It *is* windy out today, Kate! You should have seen *your* hair when you walked in!"

I got right to the point. "Forget the hair and the wind, girls. What's wrong, Patty? I know you didn't get us together to shoot the breeze!" *Geez! Wind! Breeze!* I sounded like I was being a wise guy.

Patty didn't seem to notice my comment, or if she did, she chose to ignore it. "I might as well get right to the point. I think Dave is cheating on me."

Three simultaneous gasps followed her statement. I didn't know Dave very well, so it was difficult for me (actually, for all of us) to vocalize whether or not Patty's accusation could be true. Being the friends we were, though, I knew we would try to console her anyway, while negating her suspicions.

"What makes you say that?" asked Barb. "I'm sure it's not true. Dave would never do that to you."

"Unless you caught him! Did you catch him?" asked Kate. "That dirtbag! How could he?"

"Kate! Give her a chance to talk," I reprimanded, and then turned to Patty. "Why don't you tell us what happened, and we'll keep quiet until you're finished." I gave Kate her second "shut your mouth" look. We knew that Kate meant well. She just had a hard time keeping her thoughts to herself. The truth was that Kate really liked to talk—*a lot!*

Patty ran her hands haphazardly through her hair. No wonder it looked the way it did! This was what Patty did when she was nervous; judging by her hairdo, I had to believe that she was super-stressed out.

She began, "It all started around Christmastime. I didn't want to say anything to you girls at first because I thought maybe I was overreacting. Now I don't think so." She hesitated and took a sip of her coffee. "I had this feeling that he was dividing the holidays between someone else and me. It was as if I had a Dave-imposed designated amount of time to spend with him. Sometimes, when I called him, he would hurry me off the phone, and then when he was with me, his phone was always within his reach, and he'd rush to grab it if it rang. He'd say it was business-related and go into another room to talk. One time, when he was in the bathroom and had forgotten to take his cell with him, I checked it quickly. Nothing! He had erased all incoming and outgoing calls! Now *that* really made me suspicious! And that's it in a nutshell. Well, almost it. There's one more thing." Patty blushed.

Kate, whose face was even redder than Patty's and somewhat resembled a blowfish, finally couldn't hold it in any longer. "So, *spit it out, girl!* Please tell me you're not pregnant! I'm really starting to dislike this Dave character!"

"No, I'm not pregnant. That's sort of the final issue. I can't be pregnant because we haven't had sex yet! I mean…it's been over five months already. It's just not normal!"

Barb finally spoke up again. "It certainly sounds like he's seeing someone else. What else could it be? Did you ask him?"

"No," responded Patty. "I'm afraid to hear the answer. I don't know if I *want* to hear the truth. What if he thinks I'm ugly and undesirable? I am you-know-how-old. Maybe my aging body turns him off. I don't think I could handle it if that's the case!"

"Patty," I said, "You're in the best shape of the four of us! You have the skin of a thirty-year-old. You're a beautiful woman. I seriously doubt that's the reason, but you're right. There's something going on, and we need to find out what that reason is."

"I'm in," said Barb.

"Anything for Patty," added Kate. "Besides, I'm sensing a Dave-related adventure in our future!"

"Thanks! I don't know what I'd do without you! What do you have in mind, Jill?" asked Patty.

I answered Patty's question with a counter-question. "How do you ladies feel about sleuthing, and what night next weekend is everyone available?"

"Sleuthing," breathed Kate softly as if she was already in detective mode. Her big green eyes were like those of a child ready to open her biggest Christmas present. "That sounds exciting and mysterious!"

Without further ado, Patty whipped out her ever-handy datebook, and after some schedule rearranging, we decided to meet back here on Friday night at seven o'clock.

We finished our drinks and waved good-bye to our café friends as we headed out to our cars. Just as I started to open my door, I remembered one very important detail, so I yelled out to the three retreating backs, "I forgot something!" I swear, it was strange, but I really thought that they all turned in unison. "Wear all black, including black hats!" After Barb, Kate, and Patty nodded and waved that they had heard me, I got into my car, deep in thought about my upcoming game plan.

CHAPTER 17—SHOPPING WITH
THE NOODLES

I'd never gone grocery shopping with senior citizens before, so I was a little unsure of myself on my first day of
"work." It took me an hour Monday morning just to decide on an outfit. What *does* one wear to shop with clients? I finally decided on dark jeans and a navy turtleneck, once again with a bright scarf, only this time in red.
I tied my hair back in a ponytail so my hair wouldn't get
into the Noodles' groceries. I didn't want to get fired on
my first day for contamination. I left the house thirty
minutes early, even though they only lived five minutes
away.

I thought perhaps Mrs. Noodle had ESP, because she
was already looking out the window when I arrived, and I

could see that she also had her coat on. No sooner had I stopped the car than their garage door rose, revealing a ready-to-go Mr. Noodle and the cleanest garage I had ever laid eyes upon. There were actually red-and-white checked curtains on the small windows. I got out of my car, as I seriously needed to take a closer look to see if my eyes were playing tricks on me. Nope! They weren't! The Noodles' carless garage was cleaner than the inside of my house. I had to control my impulse to jump back in my car, race home, and furiously clean!

"Hello, dear," came Gertrude's voice from beside me. I had been so focused on the immaculate garage that I'd temporarily forgotten about my clients. "Do you like the garage? I washed the floors as soon as our children took away the car."

She looked sad for a moment, but she brightened when I responded, "You did a beautiful job, Mrs. Noodle!" I couldn't believe I was standing there complimenting someone on a room that was meant to house a vehicle! Yikes!

"Please call me Gertrude or Gertie, and call him Ed," she said, pointing to her husband. "Actually, it really doesn't matter what you call him because he won't hear you anyway. Stubborn man will not wear his hearing aid!"

As if on cue, Mr. Noodle, who had been rearranging some screwdrivers, said, "Huh? Are you talking to me? I'm not deaf, you know!" Mrs. Noodle turned to me and gave me a "see what I mean?" look. Well, I think that's what it meant.

We piled into my car. Mrs. Noodle sat in front and

Mr. Noodle in back. Two blocks into the trip, Ed made me turn around and go back to check if the garage door was closed, despite my assurances that it was. Gertrude just sighed, so I supposed this was an ordinary occurrence. When we arrived at the house, he got out of the car and tried the garage handle to make sure it was locked. Gertrude once again sighed.

Finally we arrived at the supermarket. "Stay by the car, please. I'll go get us a cart," I said and headed off to secure a shopping cart. When I returned to the car, they were both gone! Where had they gone? Maybe they hadn't heard me and went into the store? I steered my way toward the entrance, but lo and behold, there was Mr. Noodle walking across the parking lot in the opposite direction from the entrance. "Mr. Noodle," I called out, but naturally he didn't hear me, although Mrs. Noodle must have, because I heard her calling to me from the store's exit. Now, how did she wind up all the way over there? The exit was on the opposite end from the entrance. I held up my hand to indicate to her to wait there as I scooted over to Ed. I hooked his hand through the cart's handle as if he were a small child and headed back to the entrance. I then waved Gertie over and hooked her hand into the other side of the handle. My hormones must have started raging from the anxiety and running, because I was now sweating profusely. I was struck by a full-blown hot flash! I couldn't believe that I had almost lost two elderly people on my first day on the job! *I had raised a child, for heaven's sake!* I should be good at this.

"Is everything OK, Jill? Your ears are bright red, and you're gritting your teeth! Do you have a fever? Maybe we should go home and come back tomorrow," said Mrs. Noodle.

Tomorrow? No way! I looked skyward and pleaded, *Please grant me the strength!* I answered her, "I'm fine, just a little warm with my coat on. Why don't we get started?"

Two hours and three Noodle-induced hot flashes later, we were finished. All I could think about was a shower and a glass of wine, not necessarily in that order. I looked at the store clock and saw that it was only three. I never drank that early, but I was beginning to think that grocery-shopping days might count as exceptions to the rule. Besides, by the time I got home, it would be close to four, so it wasn't too early. Right?

I was so anxious to get home that I packed up the car, quickly drove back to the Noodles' home, unloaded the car, *and* carried all of the groceries inside. Gertrude wanted me to stay for afternoon tea, but I rapidly declined and just as rapidly drove home, praying that all of the cops were on their doughnut breaks while I was on the road. I knew that Ed and Gertrude were upset that I had rushed them and not let them carry anything, but I told them that I was late for an appointment and would allow them to help next week. Next week! *Ugh!* I ran into the kitchen, flung open the refrigerator door, and held the wine bottle to my lips! A few more gulps and I was finally able to sit down and review my day.

The bananas and the soda were the kickers. Apparently, those were the items that Ed was in charge of, and boy, did he take his responsibility seriously! Gertrude and I had to leave him by the bananas while we continued shopping, because he needed to scrutinize every single one of the seven bananas that he required for the week. Some needed to be perfect for immediate consumption while others needed to be selected on a when-they-would-ripen basis.

After the bananas came the soda selection process. Since both he and his wife drank different brands of soda, this was also complicated. He needed to deduce exactly what they would need for the upcoming week based on what was on sale. Again, Gertrude and I left Ed alone while we completed the rest of the shopping list.

The final ordeal, which was also the cause of my third hot flash and deep desire for a drink, was the process of checking out. Ed absolutely insisted on loading the conveyor belt while Gertrude dealt with the coupon submissions and watched that all items rang up as marked. Of course, they didn't, so checkout was further drawn out. To top it all off, the Noodles would allow only the bagger to pack, as "that was his job." I wouldn't have minded except that the bagger was very slow and insisted on putting only two or three items in each bag. When he was done, our cart looked like it contained food for ten people, not two seniors who looked like they barely ate. I felt sorry for the poor cashier, who appeared to have developed a slight twitch in her left eye!

"Why are you sleeping on the kitchen table clutching a bottle of wine and murmuring something about bananas?" asked my husband two hours later when he came home from work. "Didn't you start your job today? How did it go?"

"Great!" I responded enthusiastically. If I told him

the true story, I knew he would say something to the effect of "I told you it was a crazy idea," so I just smiled at him and headed to the shower with one more positive word to him: "Perfect."

CHAPTER 18—NOT SO FUNN-IER

By Tuesday morning, I already felt the stress of my up-coming venture with Mrs. Funnier. I hadn't slept all night, and when Vic came out of the shower at 6:30 a.m., he found me sitting at the kitchen table, coffee in hand. "Would you like some?" I asked, indicating the freshly brewed, aromatic coffee.

"You do realize it's six-thirty, don't you? Do you have an appointment that I forgot about? Are you sick? Coffee smells good! I think I'll grab a cup to go." And off he went to get dressed while I continued studying the coffee in my mug, willing myself to get up and add some more to warm it up.

"Don't you have to take Mrs. Funnier shopping to-day?" Vic asked as he grabbed a thermal travel mug, filled it, and added a dollop of cream. Vic drank his coffee so dark that he might as well just drink it black. I, on the other hand, liked a creamy cup of java. "What time do you have to pick her up? Why does she shop so early?"

"She doesn't," I replied drowsily. "I couldn't sleep, so I figured I might as well get up. At the rate I'm going, I'll be ready to go back to bed right when I have to pick her up."

"You'd better go heavy on the make-up today," said Vic before he headed out the door with an added "Have fun!" I could have sworn he chuckled after that.

Have fun! Was he kidding me? I hadn't looked at myself in the mirror yet, but if Vic, who *never* commented on my appearance, insinuated that I looked bad, then I must look *really* bad! I debated going back to bed for a couple of hours, but with my luck, I'd oversleep. I didn't think Mrs. Funnier would take too kindly to tardiness.

Despite my efforts, I still dozed off on the kitchen table. Maybe I should start leaving a pillow there, because I was seriously developing some painful neck kinks. I looked at the clock and it was...*nine-thirty*! Holy moly! I had to be there in thirty minutes! I didn't even have time for a shower. Now I was going to be tired, achy, *and* smelly. I grabbed the clothes I'd worn on Monday and gave them a quick whiff. Not too bad, but just to be on the safe side, I hurried to get perfume to "freshen" them. In my haste, I slammed my hip against the doorjamb and grabbed myself in pain. "You've got to be kidding me!" I yelled to the empty air. Oliver, who must have assumed I was yelling at him, scurried under the coffee table. As usual, unknown to him, his rear end was sticking out and making him appear stuck. Actually, he looked like one of those moose heads that hunters mounted on their walls. Only, in Oliver's case, it was a cute little dog butt.

I pulled up to the senior citizen complex where Mrs. Funnier resided, and just as I had feared, there she was, standing outside and holding up her watch while pointing to it. I knew right there and then that this was not going to be a good day!

I did have a moment of suppressed humor as she stomped to the car. She was dressed in a red, knee-length down jacket and a white knit cap, which further enforced my first impression of her resemblance to a fire hydrant. Oh no! I was getting into my tired and silly mode! This would not bode well for me if I didn't gain some self-control.

As soon as she got into the car, she admonished me. "You're ten minutes late, Jill! I am a firm believer in timeliness, so please do not let it happen again, as I do not tolerate tardiness. If I can be on time, then so can you."

I had been staring straight ahead so she couldn't see the smirk on my lips, but finally I turned my head to acknowledge her. Oh no! She was sniffing the car like a dog around a hydrant. (I really couldn't get past the whole fire hydrant image.) Finally she declared, "Whatever is that smell?"

Now I started sniffing too, but I didn't smell anything. What was she talking about? Then it dawned on me! My perfume-doused, one-day-worn clothing! She was making that scrunched-up face at *me*! Quickly, I lowered all four windows and tried to nonchalantly wave the stink out of the car.

"Jill! It's freezing in here! And whomever are you waving to? There's no one in sight!"

"I'm sorry, Mrs. Funnier. I thought I saw someone I knew." I closed the windows but kept the rear ones cracked, hoping that she wouldn't notice. *With that bulky coat, how could she possibly be cold anyway?*

I parked in the lot of the same grocery store that I had been at just a mere two days ago. Mrs. Funnier seemed to be a little sharper than the Noodles, so there was no need to wrap her hand around the cart handle. At this point, I was so exhausted that I seriously contemplated sitting in the front child seat while she pushed me around. *Oops!* I felt another wave of giggles attack me, only this time I couldn't contain them!

"Jill! If you continue this odd behavior, I don't think that our relationship is going to work out! I'm an elderly woman. I can't be worrying that my helper is mentally unbalanced and may try to harm me."

"I really am very sorry," I said contritely. "I seem to not be myself today." Actually, I was acting very much like myself, and had my best friends been with me, we would have been laughing and having a grand old time in the supermarket. We probably really would have been pushing one another in the cart too!

"Well, then let's get down to business. I took the liberty of photocopying my list so we each have a copy and are on the same page."

Of course we're on the same page, I thought, looking at the neatly typed piece of paper. There was only one page to the list! I was so proud of myself. I didn't even crack a smile this time.

Mrs. Funnier had the items grouped by aisle number, with the flow beginning in the produce department, which was near the entrance, and ending at the frozen section, where we could check out close to the exit. Wow! This was a totally different shopping experience from the one with Gertrude and Ed. Matilda was quick and organized. She didn't need me. I needed her! When we were finished, I contemplated paying *her* to be *my* personal assistant.

When we arrived back at her apartment, I dutifully carried her groceries inside and offered to put them away, but she said it wasn't necessary. It was only eleven-thirty. Even with my lateness, momentary silly lapses, and two supermarket bathroom trips from all of the early-morning coffee I had consumed, we'd still completed our errand in less than one and a half hours. Mrs. Funnier might not be the most fun person to work for, but she certainly was the most time-efficient!

As I waited for her to take her coat and hat off and pay me, I looked around her living room. It was clean and organized, just like its resident. It actually felt a little too sterile, and there was an aura of loneliness to it. Her couch was plastic-enclosed like my grandparents' used to be when I was a kid. I remembered how on hot days, when I was wearing a dress or shorts, my legs would get stuck to the plastic. When I got up, I was afraid to look down for fear that I had left a layer of skin behind. For some reason, though, I didn't think that would be an issue here, as I had a distinct feeling that Mrs. Funnier didn't receive many visitors. There were pictures scattered about, but without moving up close and appearing nosy, I really couldn't tell who was in them. For all I knew, they were the pictures that were already in the frames when you purchased them. She hadn't told me much about herself other than that her husband had passed two years ago, which was when she had sold her house and relocated to the seniors' complex.

Even with the Noodles' pristine garage floor, I had felt a strong sense of happiness and family in their home, which was the same one where they had raised their children, and now their grandchildren. Plus, even with their digs at each other, I could tell that Gertrude and Ed were still in love.

I didn't get the same sense from Mrs. Funnier or her house. This saddened me. She acted independent, but I was beginning to deduce that this stoic woman was going to need me in her life as more than just an errand driver and shopping assistant; I drove away from her apartment thinking that Matilda Funnier was going to need me as a friend.

CHAPTER 19—THE MEETING

Friday was Matilda's designated banking day, but Gertrude called me last night and asked if I could take her
and Ed to the bank on Friday too. So now I was in a
"pickle" (as I liked to refer to my problems). I could either make two separate bank trips, which was probably
the more professional choice, or I could combine my clients, since they did bank at the same establishment. That
option would save me considerable time. This evening
was sleuthing night with the girls, and I needed to perfect
my game plan. I had originally anticipated having most of
the afternoon to myself, but that wasn't looking feasible
now.

I steeled myself to call Matilda to inquire if she
would be comfortable with the arrangement. She an-

swered on the first ring. Had she been standing right there, or had she run to answer the phone? I guessed she had caller ID because she said, "Good morning, Jill. I hope you're not calling to cancel. I'm all ready to go. I would hate to get dressed up for nothing."

All ready? Dressed up? I looked down at my bathrobe. At least someone was ready, but it certainly wasn't me! I hoped I hadn't gotten the time wrong.

"No, Mrs. Funnier. I'm not calling to cancel. I was just wondering if you would mind if I drove you and my other clients, Mr. and Mrs. Noodle, to the bank at the same time. I don't want to impose on you, but I have some afternoon plans of my own, and this would save me time. Of course, it's up to you."

There was a long dead silence, and I began to wonder if she had heard me or if we had been disconnected. I was just about to repeat my request when she finally blew out a breath and spoke, "I suppose that would be fine. Just this one time though. I'm not paying you to have to share my time with these other people. I'll see you in exactly one hour." And with that, she hung up.

I decided I'd better get a move on and pick up the Noodles first, as they would take the longest to get settled into the car, and I didn't think Mrs. Funnier would be patient if she had to witness Ed's leaving-the-house routine. I gave Gertrude a quick call and told her I'd be there in forty-five minutes.

As anticipated, Ed gave his house a thorough onceover before we left. Then again, as on Monday, he made me double back for a garage door and lock re-check. I realized that from now on, I was going to have to factor

in those extra minutes, especially if the Noodles had a
doctor's appointment that required punctuality.

Gertrude was in an upbeat, talkative mood this morning. I think she was happy to have someone other than Ed
to gab with, and someone who could actually hear her.
She said that she was excited to meet Mrs. Funnier and
was hoping the two women could become good friends.

Don't count on it, I thought.

As on Tuesday, Matilda was dressed and waiting
outside. She had traded the red jacket for a black wool
coat. I guessed that this was her "dress-up" coat. It was
dark-colored and straight and definitely more flattering
than the down one. She must really take her banking seriously!

Before I had time to stop her, Gertrude was out of
the car and (oh no) hugging Matilda while exclaiming,
"I'm so happy to meet you, Mrs. Funnier," which, even
worse, she pronounced "Funn-ier"! Poor Mrs. Funnier
looked like a doe caught in the headlights. She stood rigid
with her eyes wide open and a shocked expression on her
face!

To top it all off, a laughing Ed said, "That's my girl!
She welcomes everyone with open arms!"

I jumped out of the car, and in my haste to separate
the two women, I rammed my head against the top of the
door. Now I knew what the expression "to see stars"
means! I really saw hundreds of little white stars swirling
around my head as I uttered, "*Shit!*"

Uh-oh! Gertrude stopped her bear hug attack on Matilda, and both women turned to me, one with a look of
concern and the other with an even bigger look of shock

than she had already been wearing. Normally, I would have immediately apologized, but I already felt a painful lump forming on my forehead as I swayed back and forth.

"Hurry, Matilda!" yelled Mrs. Noodle. "Get ice fast! Jill's hurt!" She hurried over to me. "Are you all right, dear? I heard that! You might have a concussion! You need to come inside and lie down." She once again hollered to a still-in-shock Mrs. Funnier, "Matilda! Why are you still standing there? Open that door! We need to get Jill inside!" To my utter astonishment, the other senior finally came out of her trance and heeded the command. Then again, maybe at this point I was delusional.

With Mrs. Noodle fussing over me, I wobbled into Matilda's living room and allowed Gertrude to push me down onto the sofa, which made loud, protesting, crackling-plastic noises at my intrusion. Mrs. Funnier brought me an ice-filled dishtowel and placed it on my ever-expanding bump. She seemed to have forgotten her recent indignation as both women discussed whether I had a concussion and needed to go to the hospital.

I closed my eyes for a while until I heard double exclamations of "Don't go to sleep!"

"Where's Ed?" I asked. I hadn't seen the male senior since he was laughing in my backseat.

Gertrude said, "Knowing Ed, he fell asleep. I'll run out and crack the windows so he gets some air. He's so forgetful that later on I'll tell him we went to the bank, and he'll believe me."

"The bank," I said. "Let's go! I totally forgot." Maybe I did have a concussion after all!

"Don't worry," responded Mrs. Funnier. "We can go next week." OK. Now I *knew* I was delusional! Mrs. Funnier was being nice to me! I thought I even saw a slight smile on her blurry face, although it could have just been my eyes playing tricks on me. Gertrude came in after cracking the car's windows for Ed, and both women went into the kitchen, where I heard a kettle whistling. Matilda peeked in and said, "Don't close your eyes. Gertie and I are going to have a cup of tea while you relax. I would offer you some, but I don't think you're supposed to eat or drink when you have a concussion."

From the kitchen came sounds of soft conversation interspersed with low laughter, as apparently the ladies acquainted themselves over tea. I had been right about Mrs. Funnier. She really did need a friend; only it hadn't been me that she needed. Somehow the apartment was already taking on a warmer glow. Either that or I had a fever!

An hour later, I felt better and arose to inform the ladies. My head still hurt and the bump was going to be there for a few days, but the blurriness and dizziness were gone. Gertrude and Matilda said their good-byes and promised to "do this again" next Friday. I was a little scared about that, but I kept my mouth shut.

When we got to the car, Ed was snoring, just as Mrs. Noodle had predicted. The windows were so foggy that my vehicle looked like a bedroom on wheels. Quietly, she and I got in and drove to their home. When we pulled up to the garage, Ed finally awoke and asked, "Gertie? Did I doze off? I can't remember. Are all of our accounts in order?"

"Yes, dear," replied Gertrude, and with a wink at me added, "Everything's just fine."

CHAPTER 20—INCOGNITO

As I dressed in my head-to-toe black outfit, sans bright scarf, I studied the new addition to my head. I had iced it well when I arrived home, and it was receding somewhat, but I didn't think I'd be able to wear the baseball cap that I had originally planned on donning. A stretchy knit hat was going to have to suffice. I laced up a pair of comfortable black sneakers, put on a black down jacket, and I was ready.

A few minutes later, I waited for my friends inside of Starbucks and debated ordering a cup of coffee. On the one hand, I could use the caffeine to wake me up and ease my headache. On the other, it was going to make me have to pee while on our mission. Oh well. The coffee won. I'd just have to make sure that we stayed near a bathroom. Even when she drank nothing, Kate continuously had to urinate, so I didn't think my coffee was going to severely disrupt our activities.

One by one, they arrived, all similarly dressed in black. Leave it to Patty to look the prettiest in her long, belted wool coat with a scarf tied around her head and dark glasses. She looked like she had just finished filming a James Bond movie. The spy look definitely suited her.

They left their cars in the lot, saw me with coffee, and decided to get some for themselves. By 7:30 p.m., we were on the road. I had to borrow Vic's black sedan, as none of us drove dark-colored cars and we wanted to remain as inconspicuous as possible.

"So can you finally reveal our destination?" asked Barb from the backseat. "I've been thinking about this all week! What's with all the secrecy?"

I responded, "If I told you what I had in mind, Patty might have tried to wiggle out of it, so I thought this was the best way." I hesitated as I turned onto the highway, then continued, "We're driving into the city, and we're going to stake out Dave. I checked, and the florist shop closes at nine. Patty said that he always works on Fridays because it's so busy. That's supposed to be the main reason that their dates are on Saturdays. We're going to see exactly what Dave does when he gets out of work tonight, and if he goes straight home as he claims to our friend here." I quickly looked at Patty for confirmation, and she nodded. "Do we all understand the plan?" More nods. "Any questions?"

Naturally, Kate was the first to speak up. "This is so exciting! *That Dave* doesn't know who he's screwing with! Oops! Sorry, Patty! I meant not screwing! Never mind. You know what I meant."

"I feel like we're thirteen again and back in the cleaning closet," laughed Barb.

Patty was the last to chime in. "I'm nervous. I know you think this is an exciting adventure, Kate, but it's also my life that's going to be affected if I don't like what I see. And speaking of seeing, what if Dave spots us? What then? Do I just say 'Oh hi, Dave. We were just passing by, all dressed in black with our hair tucked out of sight.' Speaking of hair and hats, whatever is that thing sticking out of yours, Jill?"

"What thing?" asked Kate. "I can't see anything from back here." She took off her seat belt and leaned over the front seat, trying to see my head and also partially obscuring my view of the road.

I yelled while trying to steer, "Sit down, Kate! I'll show you later. You're going to get us killed!" Barb grabbed her by the collar, pulled her back, and refastened her seat belt as if she was tending to a misbehaving child.

"You know the show *Curb Your Enthusiasm*?'" said Barb to Kate. "It should have been written about you and not Larry David!"

Kate's disruption must have temporarily distracted Patty from the mission at hand, as she was staring hard at my head now. "You didn't answer me, Jill. What happened?"

I gave the girls a blow-by-blow (literally) narrative of my outings with the Noodles and Mrs. Funnier, and by the time we were through the Lincoln Tunnel and headed downtown, they all were in tears and Kate was doing Matilda impersonations. I thought it was pretty funny that Kate chose Matilda to imitate, since Kate reminded me more of a younger version of Gertrude Noodle.

Considering it was a Friday night in the city, we made good time getting to SoHo. We drove slowly past LaRosa's Artsy Flowers, with its colorful, hard-to-miss sign that had different flowers shaped in the form of letters. Naturally, all of the *r*'s were done in roses. The sign must have cost a fortune, so I had to conclude that Dave was doing well with his business.

"I see him," whispered Patty, although I had no idea why she was whispering. I quickly glanced out the window, and sure enough, I saw him helping someone who I assumed was a customer. You really couldn't miss him in his bright pink, collared shirt. At least we knew that he was definitely working.

Just as we had been lucky with the traffic, we also were fortunate enough to find a parking space only two blocks from the shop. The second we exited the car, Kate said, "I have to pee." Barb, Patty, and I needed to go too, so we filed into a nearby chain drugstore, where the security guard standing on duty at the door stopped us for questioning. I supposed that our all-black attire gave us something of a middle-aged gang appearance, although I didn't know exactly what he thought we were going to do, except perhaps knock the cashier over the head and run out with an armful of Depends! After informing us that we could only use the restroom if we made a purchase, we dutifully got in the long line and each bought a piece of candy. The sugar purchases were a good idea anyway. We probably were going to need all of the energy that we could muster for what might turn out to be a long night.

Half an hour later, we were huddled in a doorway across the street from LaRosa's. It was chilly and windy, so the opening offered some degree of shelter. Clustered together as we were, I thought we looked like praying nuns. I wondered, *If I held my cap out, would people put money in it?* Never mind. The second head growing out of my forehead might scare the Good Samaritans away! We couldn't afford to have people running from us and screaming. That would definitely blow our cover!

Surprisingly, none of us owned a pair of binoculars, so I had brought my camera with the long-distance lens as a substitute. Barb had the best eyesight, so she was appointed the lookout person.

"He just locked up," she observed. Apparently Barb was taking her duty seriously as we waited…instead of making up stories in her mind as I was, or playing Angry Birds on her iPhone as Kate was, or reapplying her lipstick as Patty was. What a wretched group of detectives we were, but that's what happened when you were fifty and easily distracted.

"So, what now?" asked Patty. "Do we follow him? He lives a mile away. Depending on the weather, he either walks or takes a train to and from work."

"Let's hope he's walking," replied Barb, "because here he comes!"

"Everyone assume your positions," ordered Kate, which earned her questioning looks from the rest of us. "You know what I mean! Get ready to move! He's coming out! *Duck!*"

The four of us hit the ground as if we were in military training. Apparently, we had all gotten As in school for following directions.

The truth was that we looked like four fools squatting in the doorway, but at least now I knew where the term "squatter" came from. "Get up," I said. "He can't see us. Plus, he's on the move!"

We followed unsuspecting Dave, staying about half a block behind him and on the other side of the street lest he turn around and spot us.

"He's going in the wrong direction," said Patty. "He just passed the main block that leads in the direction of his apartment. Where is he going? Now I'm nervous. I don't know if I want to do this anymore."

Still moving, I replied, "We can stop if you really want to. It's up to you. But it's also up to you whether you want to know the truth about your boyfriend. If we don't finish this, you're always going to wonder. You know I'm right."

Patty didn't reply, but just nodded her head in agreement, so we continued on our mission. I really hoped for my friend's sake that Dave was going to a store, and not doing what I suspected he was up to.

"Uh-oh! He's stopping at that brownstone," whispered Kate in what I guessed was her conspiratorial voice. She pointed to a house where Dave was currently ascending the outside steps. "What do we do now?"

"We wait. Right, Jill?" said Barb, never taking her eyes off the figure in the distance. "My question is how *long* do we wait?" At this point, the four of us were cold and shivering. Even I, the mastermind behind this adventure, was starting to have my doubts about what we were doing.

I told the girls, "I'm going to go get the car. Hopefully, I'll be able to find a space on this block when I drive back so we can sit and get warm. As far as how long we're going to stay here, I would imagine that's up to Patty to decide. If he doesn't come back out, we'll have to decide how to proceed. Why don't you discuss it while I'm gone? Just call me if he goes on the move again so I'll know where to meet you."

Kate fell into stride with me, saying over her shoulder, "I'll keep Jill company. I spotted a Starbucks on our way over here, and I'm going to bring back hot coffees to warm us up. I have to go to the bathroom again too."

It took Kate and me about forty-five minutes to return with the car and coffees. Dave had not exited the building yet, so we spent another ten minutes circling the street in search of a spot. We finally located one a block away from the entrance. As long as someone manned the camera, we could keep a close watch for activity.

For the next half hour, we talked about nonsense topics to pass the time, and then we fell quiet. It was after eleven, and the 39ers were pooping out.

Finally, Patty said, "We're going to have to leave eventually. We can't stay here all night. It's eleven-twenty. Let's give him until eleven-thirty, then we head home." Even I had to agree with her. As reluctant as I was to give up, eventually we were going to have to call it quits.

"He's leaving!" yelled Kate so loudly that we all screamed. She was sitting in the front seat since going to get the car, so I received the full impact of her high, piercing voice! I took off my hat and whacked her with it, and she giggled. "That sure is one ugly eye you have sticking out of your forehead! Is that your third eye? I've heard about those!"

"Yeah, Kate. It is," I responded, "and it's giving you the evil eye!"

"Be quiet, you two," scolded Patty. "He stopped on the stairs. I think someone called out the window to him because he's looking up. Wait! Now that person's coming out, too!"

Four pairs of eyes stared at the scene unfolding. Patty grabbed the camera from Kate, although I didn't think she needed it. If I could see, then so could she. I think she wanted to truly verify that what we were witnessing was what we thought it was. After a couple of minutes, Patty put the camera down and said to me in a toneless voice, "Please drive home, Jill. And...no talking."

CHAPTER 21—A NIGHT
TO REMEMBER

We pulled into a dark and almost vacant Starbucks parking lot. Without a word, Barb, Kate, and Patty got out,
climbed wearily into their own vehicles, and headed
home. I could still feel the lingering melancholy silence
that had occupied the sedan for the last forty-five
minutes.

I didn't even wash my face when I got in. I was still
chilled from the physical and mental frostiness of the
evening, so I put on my coziest sleepwear and crawled
into bed with Vic, who immediately awakened. "So," he
asked, cuddling up to me, "how did it go?"

Oliver, who had been sleeping with Vic, also woke
up and was ready for playtime. He jumped over and on

the two of us while growling and barking, and then he jumped off the bed, grabbed my slipper, and started flinging it in the air. Since this was his nightly ritual, I didn't have the heart to ignore him. Despite my gloomy mood, I followed our routine, saying, "Oliver, can you please get my slipper?" I waited patiently for him to throw it a few more times, finally plopping it back down in its original spot, so I could respond as I picked him up, "Thank you, Oliver!" Only then was he satisfied, so exhaustedly he collapsed and immediately conked out in between us. I guessed my cuddling time was also over.

Finally, I was able to recap the evening's events for my husband from the fun beginning to the sad end.

"I don't know what to say," said Vic. "So all this time, Dave's been seeing another guy? Dave's gay? Then what the heck is he doing dating Patty? What kind of jerk does that?" Vic was voicing aloud what my friends and I had been thinking on the ride home.

"I'm sure those are a few of the questions she's been asking herself since we saw him. She was devastated, Vic! She didn't say a word, but you could see it. Her face crumpled when she saw them kiss. It was so sad. And Barb, Kate, and I didn't know what to say or do. We were just as shocked as she was. Then, on the way home, she refused to talk, so none of us spoke, including Kate!" After a few more minutes of commiserating over my friend, Vic fell back to sleep.

Oliver, ever the mood sensor, opened his eyes briefly and gave me a kiss. Sometimes I swore that he was part human. Within moments, the two guys were snoring, one very softly and the other not so softly. It didn't matter, though. I knew that I was destined for a restless night, anyway.

Surprisingly, I managed to get a few hours of rest and actually slept until ten o'clock. I must have been out like a light, because I never heard either Vic or Oliver get up. I thought about calling Patty but then decided it would be better if I just went over to her condo. At first, I didn't think that she was home as I repeatedly rang the doorbell with no response. I finally called her from my cell phone, and she answered, so I told her to open the door and let me in. I wasn't leaving until I could talk to her.

Wisely, I had picked up four large cups of coffee, two for each of us. I knew we would need them after a late and sleepless night, and I also figured I could always use them as a bribe if I needed to.

I was shocked when I saw Patty, and very glad that I had decided to come over and not simply telephone her. She appeared not to have slept at all. I didn't even think she had gone to bed, as her hair wasn't mussed and her make-up was still smudged. I could tell that much of it must have been washed and wiped away by tears, not a pillow. She still had on a black sweater but had ex-changed her jeans for black sleep bottoms. Patty looked like she was in mourning, and I supposed, in a way, she was.

I didn't know if she was ready to talk yet, so I hand-ed her a coffee and enveloped her in a big hug. It was the best I could do right now.

"I think I'm all cried out for the moment," she said as we sat at the kitchen table. "I want to talk about it, but

I don't want to talk about it. What am I supposed to say other than that I'm the biggest loser at picking men? It's not *his* fault. It's mine! Stop shaking your head, Jill. You know it's true. I mean really? A gay guy? I couldn't even choose someone who was straight this time! I've officially hit an all-time low." She wiped her eyes with the wet, make-up-stained tissues in her hand, but it must have been from habit because she wasn't crying. "And I'm serious about not wanting to talk about it. There's nothing to say. Dave's gay, and for whatever warped reason, he still chose to date me. Unless he's bisexual, but even then he should have told me. Now I have to deal with breaking up with him when he comes here tonight, and I honestly would prefer to never lay eyes on his lying, cheating face again!"

"Do you want me to be here when he comes?" I asked. I would do anything for my friend, including breaking up with and telling off her gay boyfriend. "I know it's a teeny consolation, but now you know why he wasn't interested in sex and you can stop blaming yourself. It also explains why he never got married. He's been feeding you line after line of bull all this time!" When I saw Patty's expression, I stopped talking. "Sorry. I'm supposed to be keeping my mouth shut. Just tell me what you want me to do, and I'll do it."

"There's nothing you can do," she responded. "I appreciate your being here now, and I appreciate your idea for last night's trip, even though it ended badly. If we hadn't gone, who knows when I would have found out the truth? I really liked him, Jill, but at least I didn't love him! I don't even know if I'm capable of love anymore. I feel like the older I get, the less interested I am in making someone else the number one in my life. Let's face it; I've been my own number one for fifty years. Do I really want to share that focus with another person?"

I thought about what Patty had said. I could understand perfectly what she meant, and I told her as much. "Relationships are a lot of work. Most of the time I don't even realize it until Vic and I go through a rough period and it becomes obvious. Problems don't necessarily work themselves out on their own. You have to make a conscious attempt to fix them. Couples are always evolving and changing, within themselves and within their relationship, so the work is constant. I hope I'm making sense here?"

I looked at Patty, and she nodded, saying, "I do understand. I've been single for so many years that I don't think I can or even want to adjust my life to someone else's. My childbearing years are over, so there's never going to be a baby in my future. I thought about this a lot last night. I guess I'm learning some things about myself that I never realized until now. Or maybe I'm just facing reality. Am I being selfish, Jill?"

I shook my head no as I picked up my second cup of coffee and walked over to the microwave to reheat it. The phone rang, and I heard Patty say, "Hi, Barb," so I gestured to her to stay on the phone and waved good-bye, whispering to her to call me if she needed me later on. She already appeared to be much better than when I had arrived, but tonight's confrontation was going to be tough for her, regardless of her new relationship viewpoint.

When I returned home, I sat at my own kitchen table

for a while, thinking about what my friend and I had discussed. Whenever the single people I knew encountered dating problems, I always felt renewed gratitude for my husband. After almost twenty-five years of marital ups and downs, we were still very much in love and continued to have a great time together. Also, we had this wonderful son as a result of our union, and I wouldn't have changed *that* for anything in the world! I was fifty and extremely content with my life. I truly hoped that Patty would continue to feel as she did today and learn to become comfortable with the way her life had turned out. She didn't have to get married to avoid loneliness, as she would never be alone. She would always have Barb, Kate, and me, just as we would always have her.

CHAPTER 22—SICK

"Oh, poor me! I hate being sick! My whole body aches and my throat is sore and my nose won't stop running! Can you see if I have a fever?" I moaned to Vic from under the covers as he got ready for work, barely glancing in my direction. At one point, he walked toward me and bent over, and I thought that he was going to give me a hug or something just as sweet, but then he reached down and grabbed his shoes from under the bed, and my illusions were shattered.

It was the Monday after that fateful Friday Dave fiasco, and I thought I'd caught a cold that night. I'd started sneezing and sniffling yesterday, and I was already in full-blown cold mode this morning, which didn't bode well for me. When viruses hit me this hard and this fast, I was sure to be down for the count for a good week. I let out a small moan that went ignored by my dear husband.

When he was finished getting dressed, Vic came over, put his hand on my forehead so briefly that it felt like a soft breeze on my face, and said, "You feel fine. I have to go. See ya later. Hope you feel better." And off he went.

Yup! That was my husband, Mr. Compassion! Sympathy just oozing out of every pore. Most of the time, I didn't let it bother me, but when I felt this bad, it really irked me. Oliver had more compassion than Vic. He was cuddled up to my side, sharing his soft doggy warmth. Granted, he'd do this even if I wasn't sick, but I liked to think that I was getting a little extra TLC from my buddy this morning.

Vic had so many redeeming qualities that in the grand scheme of things, this wasn't the worst way he could act, but I was still annoyed. When he was sick or in pain, he made sure I knew about it, and I think I always gave the proper amount of sympathy, even empathy if the situation called for it.

I thought about the time when I was seven months pregnant. I had awakened early on a Saturday morning with one of Neil's appendages "stuck" somewhere in my left side. It felt like my uterus had sprouted an arm or a leg! I couldn't move! I woke Vic up as I cried in pain, and his response was, "I have to meet my brother in thirty minutes to play golf."

I'd sobered up quickly at that statement and looked at him in shock. Was he kidding me? Golf? I was in excruciating pain from his unborn child and he wanted to go play *golf*! What was I supposed to do? Lie here and wait for him to come home?

I felt the steam coming out of my ears, and I let him have it! "*So*," I cried, "golf is more important to you than your wife's pain? Do I mean nothing to you? Don't you love me? How could you leave me like this to go play golf?" I was getting a little hysterical at this point, but I did have the whole hormonal thing going on, or at least that was what I told myself to excuse my overdramatic behavior.

After about ten minutes of back-and-forth bickering over whether or not he should leave, Vic finally relented and stayed home with me. I knew it wasn't because of my suffering and his supreme sympathy for me, but rather that he didn't want to listen to me complain about it afterward if he did go. A pregnant woman could take perceived injustices to new lengths and always have the element of hormones on her side. She could devise all forms of torturous retributions during those endless sleepless nights. I think the part of Vic's brain that centered on self-preservation must have taken over when he made the decision to defer to my wishes.

I continued to lie there this morning with the covers pulled up to my nose and Oliver twitching and snoring beside me, and I realized that I was seriously feeling sorry for myself. I needed someone to cheer me up, and I knew exactly who to call.

I got up, wrapped myself in my fluffy turquoise robe that I thought enhanced my green eyes (even though no one but Vic and Neil saw me in it), and headed downstairs to make myself tea. For me, tea was reserved for times of illness, like chicken soup or plain crackers.

While the tea brewed, I decided to put in a call to my brother. It was still a little too early, but I figured I could leave a message, and he'd get back to me when he was awake and ready to talk. Anthony's job required him to drive throughout the day, so in between jobs I was hoping that he could stop by for a pick-*me*-up. My brother was a bug man by day and a self-proclaimed scientist in his off hours. This basically meant that he exterminated all manner of insects and rodents as a means to make a living. When he wasn't working, his spare time and energy went into completing the perfect invention that would amass him fame and fortune. Thus far, that hadn't happened yet, but Anthony never let his failures deter him. He just formed a new idea and forged ahead with it.

True to his nature, my predictable brother returned my call. His loud, ebullient voice shot through the phone (and through my aching head): "Hey, Sis! What's going on? You're sick? What's wrong?"

For a second, I considered telling him to never mind, that all was well and I felt much better, but my misery won out and I replied, "Can you come over this afternoon? I'm sick and could use a little cup of cheer. Actually, some Starbucks would be nice, too. Maybe it would clear up my nose because it's been running like crazy."

"Don't let it run too far or Oliver might get it and chew it up! Ha-ha-ha-ha-ha!" He laughed very loudly into my ear. My silence must have conveyed my lack of amusement because he quieted down. "I have a job in your area before lunch, so why don't I pick us up a couple of coffees and something to eat, and I'll swing by?"

"Thanks, Anthony! You're the best! One more fa-
vor? Please don't tell Mom that I'm sick."

"Sure. Sure. No problem. I'll see ya in a few hours."
He disconnected.

I figured that even though it was only my brother
coming, I should make myself halfway presentable,
meaning I had better take a shower. I grabbed my second
cup of tea and headed off to the bathroom. I looked in the
mirror and screamed! Poor Oliver, who had still been
asleep on the bed, jumped up and began barking. "Shh," I
said to him "Mommy just scared herself for a minute. It's
all better now." My dog, after giving me what appeared
to be a dirty look, repositioned himself on the comforter
and promptly returned to his slumber.

I hazarded another glance in the mirror and was appalled by my supernaturally white face, accentuated by a
bulbous red nose and puffy, bloodshot eyes. Literally
topping off the horrid picture were frizzy strands of
brown hair standing out in all directions. My flattering
robe was definitely not working for me today!

The warm shower put me in a cozy, sleepy mood, so
I hit the hay for a couple of hours before Anthony's arrival. With the exception of a quick let-out for necessary
bathroom functions, Oliver was happy to jump right back
into bed with me for some more snoozing and cuddling.
It was like mommy/doggy quality time.

An hour later, the phone rang, and I grabbed it,
thinking that it was Anthony. It wasn't. It was my mother. I considered pretending that I was my answering machine, but I didn't think she was gullible enough. "Hi,
Mom. What's up?"

"Your brother called me and said you were sick! Why didn't you call me to come over?" she admonished me. "Did Vic stay home?"

I rolled my eyes. "No, Mom. Vic is not going to miss work to care for his sick wife. I'm a big girl now."

"Well, you called Anthony, didn't you? He said you wanted him to come over with coffee. I could have brought you coffee. Not that stuff you like so much, though. It's way too strong and bitter! Anyway, you never want me to help you, Jill. Why is that?"

I hesitated to respond. I could whack my sibling upside the head for telling our mother. He knew how she got when she felt unneeded, and I had specifically told him *not* to tell her! Now I had to make up a story to appease her. Telling Mom that I hadn't called her because her presence would drive me insane didn't seem to be the way to go. "I called Anthony because I wanted him to set up a few of those humane mouse traps. Yes. That's why I called him. There was no need for the both of you to visit." I nodded my head. That was fast thinking for a sick woman, but just in case she didn't believe me, I added, "I think I'm starting to feel better already."

"Hmm." I heard her in thinking mode. "I'll be home all day if you need me. Just lock that dog up if you change your mind. He's too wild, and I don't want him jumping all over my winter white pants."

"OK, Mom. No problem. Speaking of 'that dog,' I think he has to go out. Talk to you later." I hung up. Leave it to Mom to nicely offer her help and then ruin it by bashing my precious Oliver.

At twelve o'clock, the doorbell rang and the knocker

sounded in tandem. My brother got a kick out of making as much of a ruckus as possible to announce his arrival.

"What a bro," I said when I saw him. As promised, he had brought me a Starbucks coffee and one of their delicious desserts to go with it. "You're lucky you brought the coffee, though, because I wasn't happy about you calling Mom. I told you not to call her! I swear, Ant, I really wonder if you listen to people when they talk. You would have been in trouble if she had showed up at my front door!"

"Sorry, Sis! I called to ask her something, and I let it slip. I swear, it will never happen again!"

We sat down at the kitchen table and chatted for a while, but I could see he was trying to contain his excitement over something. "OK. Spit it out! I know there's something you want to tell me. Another blond girlfriend, perhaps?"

"Jill! Don't you know? There's *always* a blond girlfriend." He laughed. "But no, that's not it. I have a little surprise for you."

Oh no! Anthony's surprises were never a good thing. I was a little scared to hear or see what this bombshell would be! At least, I knew it wasn't a blond bombshell!

He grabbed the paper bag that he had placed on the table when he came in, and opened it up. "When you said you had a runny nose, I thought this would be the perfect time to unveil my latest creation! Are you ready?" he asked excitedly. "Close your eyes!"

No way was I closing my eyes, and I told him as much. Some things needed to be done with one's eyes open, and this was one of those things!

"Voilà," Anthony exclaimed as he pulled out what appeared to be mini tampons. "They're my new invention! I call them Nosepons! What do you think? Try one! Stick it up your nose!"

Being the good-sport sister that I was, I tentatively took one and stared at it nervously. Anthony's inventions had been known to explode, so I was a tad hesitant to place this latest one up my nose or anywhere else in my body.

"Go for it," he urged. "You'll never have to worry about a runny nose again. I even made them in different sizes! Also, scented and unscented! How cool of an idea is this?"

Actually, I really did think they were a cool idea, so I inserted what looked to be a size small, unscented Nosepon into one nostril. "Not bad," I said. "Can I try a scented one too?"

Anthony handed me one labeled "menthol," and I put it in the other nostril. I had to admit, they were more comfortable than sticking tissues or napkins up your nose, and they didn't ridiculously stick out like those did. I walked over to look in the little mirror by my sink and laughed! I definitely appeared to have two tampons hanging out of my nostrils. The strings were the kicker! I was menstruating out of my nose! Hysterical! Only my brother could have come up with this crazy invention!

"So," he asked. "What do you think? I know the strings look funny, but they make for easy removal."

"I think they're great," I responded enthusiastically, "but very funny-looking! Definitely for home use and especially for sleeping. It's one of your better inventions, though." When I saw his frown, I added, "The others were good too, but Nosepons are up there with your *really* good ideas!"

"Thanks, Jill! Now I have to come up with a marketing strategy. Do you think Vic would help me out? Talk to him, please! I have to get back to work. I'll leave you with some Nosepons for your cold. Just change them out when they're soaked through." My brother was forgetting that he was speaking to a woman, and one thing women knew how to do was handle any type of "pon"!

I was right about one thing; Anthony's visit had perked me up, just as I had expected. After turning on both the gas fireplace and the television, I grabbed Oliver and a book and plopped myself down on the couch. I was settled in for an afternoon of cold-induced relaxation.

I must have fallen asleep, because the next thing I knew, Vic stood in front of me with a strange expression.

"Jill? Why do you have tampons stuck in your nose? I thought you didn't get your period anymore? I know you've gotten forgetful, but did you truly forget where to insert a tampon?"

"They're Anthony's latest invention, and they're called Nosepons," I replied.

"I hope you realize just how strange your family is," he said, and walked away to get undressed.

Yeah, I have a strange family, I thought as I spotted my father-in-law outside my living room window, doing his end-of-the-day, check-every-window-and-door, walk-around-his-house routine. Aloud, I retorted, "And yours is normal?"

CHAPTER 23—BANKING WITH THE "CLIENTS"

Between last Friday's unexpected head injury and this week's sickness, I never took the Noodles or Mrs. Funnier to the bank, so today I would once again make the attempt, hopefully with a more successful outcome than last week's fiasco.

Before I left, I called Gertrude and asked her to have Ed lock up the house and be prepared to go when I arrived. I thought that with each week's experience, I would learn a new lesson for upcoming outings. Hopefully, I would eventually learn their habits and routines, and our jaunts would begin to run more smoothly.

The pickup and ride to the bank went efficiently. Once again, I took all three seniors in the same trip. Gertrude and Matilda must have spoken during the week because they hadn't stopped chatting since getting into the car. Mrs. Noodle even made her husband sit in the front so she could sit next to her new friend.

"I had to get an acquaintance to take me food shopping this week," complained Mrs. Funnier unhappily.

"Oh, Matilda! Be nice! Jill was sick. She couldn't help it. How are you feeling, dear?" inquired Gertrude.

"I'm better, thank you," I replied. I hoped Matilda's annoyance at my illness didn't ruin the day. At least Gertrude seemed comfortable with admonishing her.

When we arrived at the bank, the three seniors joined a rather lengthy line to wait. I sat on one of the plush chairs, situated for patrons who were waiting for the customer service employees to help them.

Mrs. Funnier was ensconced in her red down jacket again, and I could tell she was getting warm as she waited in line, so I walked over and asked her, Gertrude, and Ed if they wanted me to hold their coats. The Noodles were happy to comply, but Mrs. Funnier was getting ornery.

"No, thank you, Jill. I'm not taking my coat off, because I intend on being done here soon. I don't know why this line is moving so slowly. They never have enough tellers! I keep saying that I'm going to move my business to another bank. Maybe I should withdraw all of my money today! See how they like *that*!"

I glanced around and saw that Matilda had everyone's attention. The tellers looked at her with dread, so I assumed that this wasn't the first stink she had made here. I looked to Gertrude for help, but she just shrugged at me and took a few steps away from her friend as if to say, "No. She's not with me."

I liked Gertrude's attitude, so I decided to copy it. I returned to my chair and opened up a magazine.

"Ed? *Ed!* Come back here." I looked up and saw Ed walking toward the exit while his wife called to him from her spot in line.

"Crap," I mumbled under my breath. Who knew banking could be so stressful? I hurried over to Ed and asked, "Where are you going? We're not finished yet. Your wife is waiting for you." I looked imploringly at Mrs. Noodle, but she ignored me just as she had ignored Mrs. Funnier.

"I have to go to the bathroom," he whispered. "Do you know where it is?"

"I think it's just for the employees, Ed. Can you hold it in?"

"No," he responded. "I'm going to take a walk and see if I can find one nearby." And off he went.

"Jill!" Mrs. Noodle beckoned to me. "Where did Ed go?" When I told her, she became frantic. "He'll get lost. You have to stop him! He loses his bearings easily!"

I ran out the door and spotted Ed at the corner, entering a pizzeria. I waited outside. Ed exited the restaurant and approached me, and I heard the pizza maker yell, "Hey buddy! Next time you come in to use the bathroom, you have to buy something!" Poor hard-of-hearing Ed didn't hear him. I grabbed my client by the arm and hurried him back into the bank before the guy harassed him further.

Gertrude stepped up to one teller's window and, as luck would have it, Matilda stepped up to the other. I gave up on the idea of sitting, so I went to stand between the two ladies with Ed in tow. Mrs. Noodle rummaged through her half-empty purse. Apparently, she didn't take her transactions out until she was at the window. I saw the teller discreetly roll her eyes at the other teller.

"I'd like to make a withdrawal," Gertie finally said to the young woman, who asked her to enter her PIN number into the small black machine to the left of the window. "Oh dear. I always forget my number," she fretted. "Ed! What's our PIN number? Is it your birthday or mine?"

"*What?*" yelled Ed.

"Our PIN number! Which birthday is the PIN number?" she repeated loudly.

"Whose birthday is it?" answered a confused Ed. "Are we taking out money for someone's birthday?"

The teller, who in my opinion was being extremely patient, said, "Why don't you just try both numbers, Mrs. Noodle?"

As Gertrude entered numbers, I heard Matilda's voice: "I would like the balance on these three accounts, and I know *my* PIN, and it's *not* my birthday! Here are the account numbers." And she handed a small piece of paper to her teller.

"Mrs. Funnier, if you enter your PIN, I can pull up your accounts. I don't need the numbers."

"Yes, but mine are the correct numbers, and what if you don't pull up the correct numbers? I need to make a deposit, and I don't want you putting the money in someone else's account. I've heard about those things happening. No one's perfect," she stated, staring forebodingly at the not-so-patient teller.

I felt inclined to intervene, but then thought better of it. I had a feeling that for the Noodles and Mrs. Funnier, these were weekly occurrences. I didn't think that "teller intervention" was in my job description, and I had to believe that these girls were used to my clients' antics. If they weren't, then today would be a learning experience for all of us. Feeling justified, I returned to my chair to watch the comical scene before me. At this point, Matilda, who still had not removed her coat, was overheating. I could envision her red face and matching jacket exploding, bits of her showering down like marked money when it exploded on bank robbers. To her right, Gertrude and Ed argued over their numbers as they entered in all different numerical combinations. The manager finally asked another teller, who appeared to be at lunch, to open up her window, as the line was now wrapped around the ropes. To top it off, everyone was looking at me with exasperated expressions. This was my cue to step outside and wait. Better yet, I was going to hunker down in the car in case anyone decided to get violent.

Fifteen minutes later, the three exited the bank, looking sullen and unhappy. I wondered if they had completed their transactions, but dared not ask for fear that they would want to go back in. Since I also had my accounts here, I would probably have to do my banking in disguise from now on. Or maybe I should just switch banks to be on the safe side.

Ed finally broke the silence. "Jill, we have to return here on Monday. Before we could conclude our business, the computers started doing crazy things. I think maybe

Gertie and I screwed them up with all of the numbers we were entering. The manager said to come back Monday at five o'clock."

Without a word, I drove off, but not before catching a glimpse of an angry-looking mob departing the bank. I didn't have the heart just yet to tell my unhappy seniors that the bank wasn't open at five on Monday. They'd learn that soon enough!

CHAPTER 24—SEXUAL HEALING

By the end of February, my chauffeuring job had settled into a predictable routine—as much as seniors can be predicable, that is. There was always one problem or another, but I was becoming more adept at handling them. When the weather warmed up, maybe I would consider taking on another client. That was a big "maybe," though. Things were going well, so I wasn't sure I wanted to tempt fate by increasing my business.

It was a snowy, icy winter that showed no sign of letting up. I drove the short distance to Starbucks and observed six-foot mounds of snow everywhere. Because of the continuous bad weather, tonight would be my first time seeing the girls since our evening of Dave chasing.

Patty, dressed in head-to-toe black, was already there

when I arrived. She looked like a woman in mourning with her pale face and blond hair. I thought she might have lost weight too. The word that came to mind to describe her was "vulnerable." In the past, I never would have used that term to describe my single friend. The Dave debacle had taken its toll on her. She was definitely going to need some TLC and cheering up tonight. I was sure that Barb and Kate would also notice her condition when they arrived, so there was no need to say anything. I had no idea at that moment just how much unplanned cheering up was in store for all of us.

I hugged Patty and heard Kate's distinctive voice and Barb's softer one behind me. We exchanged hugs and kisses, and I noticed that there was a strange expression on Barb's face. Now what was that all about? I had just spoken to her yesterday, and nothing out of the ordinary had come up in the conversation. Although, now that I thought about it, yesterday was the first time we had spoken in a week, which was uncommon.

As usual, there was no conversation until we were served our beverages and comfortably seated. I began the catch-up talk with a lengthy, detailed description of my outings with the Noodles and Mrs. Funnier. The more stories I told, the louder our laughter became, enhanced by my standing and acting out the scenes I was describing. Barb seemed to be overenthusiastically jumping up and down with humor, and I once again had to wonder what was going on with her. I was happy to see that Patty was already in a better mood.

"I keep meaning to ask you," said Kate in my direction, "how did you handle Neil's return to college after the holiday break? I'm embarrassed to say this, but I was actually slightly relieved to see "Little" Lou's back when he headed out the door. I can't believe I was such a mess back in September. For the month he was home, all I did was shop for food, cook, and do laundry. The grocery bill and the gas and electric bill went sky-high for that month. Every time I walked over to the sink, there was a dish or a glass. You get the picture. And the laundry! Holy cow! All the kid did was change his clothes! How dirty can he get sitting on a sofa? Were they like this before, Jill? I can't remember."

"Yes, Kate. At least I think they were, but we probably didn't notice because we didn't have anything to compare it to. But I know what you mean. Plus, with the lousy weather, all Neil did was sit in a chair doing the usual. He'd go to bed at 4 a.m. and sleep till 2 p.m., and it started grinding me up inside! I'll deny it if you ever repeat this, but I was glad to see him go back, too! Does that make us bad mothers?"

"Nah," chimed in Patty. "The both of you just spent eighteen years devoted to your family, and now you have more time for yourselves when they're away. So, when they come home, your new routine is disrupted. No way either of you is a bad mom! I've witnessed firsthand the stuff you've done for Lou and Neil all of these years. Just the butt wiping alone should be enough for good-mother status, at least in my opinion. And I can be objective about it, since I don't have any kids of my own."

By this time, Barb was doing some serious squirming in her seat, and I couldn't keep quiet any longer. "Barb! What the heck is wrong with you tonight? Your face keeps crinkling up, and you're acting as if you have ants in your pants! You kind of look like Kate when she really has to go to the bathroom." Patty and Kate ceased talking and also turned their attention to our friend.

Barb turned beet-red. "I can't believe this, but I'm a little embarrassed to tell you." She looked around to ensure that no one was eavesdropping and whispered, "I had a vaginal rejuvenation and I'm uncomfortable right now."

"You had a *what*?" came Kate's very loud whisper.

"Shh!" said Patty. "This definitely doesn't sound like it's going to be a conversation for our fellow coffee drinkers to overhear. But I'm with Kate. What exactly is vaginal rejuvenation? I've never heard of such a thing! What do you do, go to a spa and get it spritzed with some kind of refresher? Stop looking at me like that, Barb! I'm seriously dumbfounded!"

I'd never heard of it either, so I was still perplexed over Barb's mortification. This was the girl who used to brag about everything and very rarely got embarrassed about anything.

"I'm surprised none of you have ever heard of it. I'd better start from the beginning." Barb lowered her voice. "Remember when I told you about Jerry and my New Year's disaster?" We nodded. "I started thinking that maybe I was getting too loose down there, and that was why Jerry wasn't interested in sex anymore. Two kids can do that, you know, and they were big babies, too!" She inclined her head toward her crotch, so we would get where "down there" was, like we were idiots or something. OK, maybe sometimes we *were* a little dense.

"Jill! Can stop looking at my crotch? And Kate, why are you wriggling?" asked Barb.

"I just have this feeling that it's going to be a squirmy story or a gagging story. I don't know...I guess I'm subconsciously preparing myself. Just continue," replied Kate.

Barb proceeded with her story. "I looked up this procedure because I heard two of my realtors talking about it. I found the name of a good doctor and went to see him, and he agreed that I could use a tightening."

Patty, Kate, and I were *all* squirming now. None of us liked where this tale was heading!

"Stop moving! Now you all look like you have to go to the bathroom!" We forced ourselves to stay still and waited for the forthcoming elaboration. I didn't think I even wanted to hear it anymore, but I had asked, hadn't I?

"The bottom line is that you go into the hospital for same day-surgery. You're put under anesthesia, the doctor goes in and does a little nipping and tucking, and you're good as new."

"*Argh!*" screamed Kate so loudly that people in the café actually jumped to their feet to see what had happened. She ran gagging and choking to the ladies' room, and I did one of those waves to the other patrons that meant, "Everything's OK. Go back to your drinks." When the café returned to normal, the conversation resumed.

"Are you crazy?" exclaimed Patty. "Sexy teddies are one thing, but seriously, Barb, firming up your womanhood may be taking things a little too far! I could see doing those Kegel exercises, but surgery? Really?"

"I don't want to be one of those women who get divorced because their husbands lose interest in them sexually, so I'll do anything to keep the fires burning," answered Barb.

"I understand where you're coming from, but tell me, what does *he* do to fan the flames? Sounds to me like you're the only one trying. Maybe he's not interested in sex because he's too wrapped up in his job," I said.

"Too late now. What's done is done. This is why I didn't ask your opinions before I went. I knew you would have tried to talk me out of it."

"Damn straight!" came Kate's voice from the counter, where she was awaiting a fresh coffee. She added sugar substitute and creamer and approached us. "Wanting to spice things up is fine. There are plenty of nonsurgical ways to do that. When was the last time you and Jerry went away together sans children? I'll tell you when. Never! You, Jill, and I have been married a long time. Sometimes intimacy is simply about the comfort you have with each other. You know: talking, hanging out, and doing everyday stuff together. Let's face it: we've been having sex with the same guys for a lot of years. The intense passion of the early years isn't gone; it's just different. Now it's one that's born of many years of love. I hardly think that a loose you-know-what is going to drive him into the arms of another woman." Kate finally sat down. "And that's all I have to say on the subject."

"How does it feel?" I asked. Even though the idea gave me the creeps, I was still curious. Then I laughed.

"I'd ask how exactly it was done, but I don't want to send Kate running and screaming again."

"Thank you, Jill! That would be too much information for me," said Kate.

"It's painful and itchy right now. The doctor said it would subside in a few days. Just compare it to having a bad infection." When she saw Kate's face beginning to crinkle up again, she ended the description.

"You know," began Patty, "I was down in the dumps when I first got here. I'm still trying to get over the whole Dave thing. But after listening to you girls talk about vaginal loosening and tightening and less passionate long-term sex, I have to say that maybe it's not so bad without a permanent partner. I can choose whether or not to have sex, and if the sex isn't good, I don't have to stick around. I certainly don't foresee any surgical procedures in *my* future. I don't have nor will I ever have children of my own. I'm actually pretty happy with my life, and I have great people like you three surrounding me. After Dave, I don't even know if I want to get serious anymore. If it happens, it happens, and if it doesn't, then that's OK too. I really like this whole fifty-year-old outlook on life. I feel like it took me fifty years to finally feel free." She looked at Barb, Kate, and me and asked, "Am I boring you?"

We laughed! I knew that she wasn't waiting for an answer. The fact was that it was ten o'clock, and we were yawning from weariness, not boredom. Yes, fifty was a great age for women in a lot of ways, but it didn't change the fact that we *were* getting older, and we were tired right now. Kate, Barb, Patty, and I downed the last of our drinks and headed out the door, waving good-bye to our barista friends.

Three smiling, sleepy faces kissed me goodnight, and I couldn't help noticing that Patty had regained the color and vitality in her countenance over the course of the evening. I think she was finally ready to move on with her life. Thank heavens!

CHAPTER 25—HOW "BAAD" CAN IT BE?

Gertrude had phoned me on Friday and asked if I could drive her and Ed to their doctor's office today, Tuesday, as they both had appointments for their physicals. She said that she would have told me sooner, but she forgot. I had nothing going on anyway, so I was able to take them. Their appointment was for 10 a.m., so my afternoon would remain open.

I magnanimously volunteered to stay (free of charge) and keep them company at their doctor's visit. Gertrude was thrilled. Ed said nothing.

"That would be so nice of you, Jill! Ed always sits there and doesn't talk. I get bored. Now I have you to talk to. You can even come in with me for my checkup! Usually Ed comes in with me, but I'm sure he won't mind hanging around here in the waiting room. Would you, Ed?"

"*What?*" yelled Ed.

Uh-oh and whoa! I never said anything about escorting anyone for his or her elderly-naked-body exam. I didn't even look at my own mother's bare butt, let alone my clients'!

"You know, Jill, I would really appreciate your young mind in there listening to the doctor. I try to write everything down, but I start to lag behind. Then I come home with only half the stuff written on my pad. Maybe you could write it down for me?"

Gertrude Noodle looked at me imploringly, and I didn't have the heart to say no. I nodded, but there was no way that I was gazing at her disrobed figure.

There appeared to be a few people ahead of us, so I grabbed a magazine to glance through as I chatted with Gertrude. Ed had brought a newspaper and was already deeply engrossed in the sports section.

"Why does that young boy have wires hanging out of his ears?" asked Mrs. Noodle, as she surveyed the other occupants of the waiting area. "Are those the newfandangled hearing aids that all the seniors are raving about? I gotta ask Doctor Baad for those for Ed! That boy doesn't look old enough to need them, though."

I looked across the room at the teen listening to music on his iPod and was just about to try to explain this "new" invention when she continued. "And what's that little box they're plugged into? Is that a hearing monitor? What do you do with it when you're walking around, or is it a special sitting hearing aid?"

Now, how was I going to explain to Gertrude what an iPod was? I decided to keep it as simple as possible. No sense confusing the already confused woman.

"That's a very small music player," I told her as I tried to come up with something that she could relate to. I got it! "Remember the small transistor radios from years ago that you could listen to with earphones? Well, that's the same thing, only much smaller and with very good sound. There's no music static either like on those old radios." Actually, I was pretty proud of my explanation. I was really getting the hang of communicating with old people!

Mrs. Noodle smiled and nodded her head in understanding, but then she hit me with a hard one. "Why does he keep touching it? Doesn't he know that he's going to leave fingerprints on it? Didn't his mother teach him to respect his possessions? Maybe he has that OCD disease I hear about on the talk shows! Have you ever heard of OCD, Jill? I can't remember what it stands for. It's a lot of words, I think. I'll ask Doctor Baad."

On the one hand, I was glad she had turned her attention away from the boy and was now focusing on his "disease" so I wouldn't have to explain a touch screen. But then again, I was thinking that Gertrude might have some issues of her own, as in ADD. Already she was inspecting the other patients for more abnormalities.

Before I had a chance to intervene, she called out to a heavyset woman in our row of seats, "When are you due, dear? You look ready to deliver any minute. You and the hub must be so excited!"

The young woman turned red, then purple as her face scrunched up into an unsightly, mean expression!

I put my hand on my client's shoulder to halt her, but she jumped up exclaiming, "Oh my! Is it coming now? *Nurse? Nurse!* The baby is coming!"

If I hadn't been so mortified, I would have laughed. The person in question truly did look like she was in labor. I pulled Gertie back into her chair and whispered in her ear, "Shh! She's not pregnant! She's overweight!"

Gertrude's face immediately turned the same shade as her victim's. She covered her mouth, then uncovered it, and said, "I'm so sorry, dear. Never mind."

"Mr. Noodle," came the nurse's voice over the office loud speaker. Thank God! I was saved from any further inquisitions!

"*What?*" yelled Ed again, only this time he jumped up. "What do you want?" he called out to the speaker.

"He does this every time," Mrs. Noodle said to me as she rose and took his arm. "You'd think he would be used to it by now." Then she too called out to the wall, "We're coming!"

I shrank down in my chair and tried to pretend that I wasn't with the Noodles, as I saw a laughing nurse open the reception door to usher them in.

I sat there by myself, browsing through my magazine, and it suddenly struck me: The doctor's name was Dr. Baad! Who goes to a "Baad" doctor? Oh no! The poor Noodles! Now I knew why Gertrude wanted me to go in with her. I felt *bad* for almost saying no.

Ed came out after a half hour with a huge grin on his face. "The doc says I'm fit as a fiddle! Gertie asked if you could go in, Jill. She gets nervous around docs. Beats me why! She's seen enough of them in her years! She always has some ailment or another! I told her that she needs to drink wine at night like I do. Look what it's done for me." He did a little gorilla thump on his chest.

I gave him the thumbs-up sign as I got up and headed back to Mrs. Noodle's room. I knocked on the door as I opened it a crack to make sure that she was covered, and I happily observed that she was. I looked at her in the examination gown, and for the first time saw how appropriate Gertie's last name was. I wondered if the same held true for Ed. *Yuck!* I can't believe I even thought that for a fraction of a second! Gertie had white, pasty, flabby skin and did indeed look just like a wet noodle.

While I was rubbing my eyes, trying to get that unsightly image out of my head, the doctor walked in and Gertrude introduced him to me. "Dr. Baad, this is my driver, Jill." Dr. Baad gave me a bit of a strange look, but he nodded in acknowledgement and shook my hand. I quickly positioned myself in a corner with pad and pen in hand, which earned me another queer look from the doc.

"So, Mrs. Noodle," he said, "besides your routine physical, do you have any other concerns you wish to tell me about?"

"Jill, are you getting this?" she addressed me before answering her physician. I quickly scribbled his question, so she could continue. I already was feeling a little silly, but I had agreed to do this, so there was no backing out now.

With one swift movement, Gertrude stood, pulled up the back of her gown, and exposed a very white, loosely held together rear end. *Cripes!* The room was only about four feet by four feet, and I couldn't escape! Her butt was a foot away from my face! I pressed my back into the wall, and turned my head to gaze at the one framed picture on the wall. It was just the black-and-white image of a tree, but I studied that tree like it was the most fascinating one I had ever seen.

She pointed to a spot right in the crack and said, "Doc, I feel a lump right here." To punctuate her statement, she jabbed at her crack. I was mortified, and I couldn't tell if my face was heating up from embarrassment or a hot flash!

"Gertrude, why don't I step out for a minute and leave you alone?" I said.

"Oh no, Jill dear, please stay! We're both women. Nothing to see that you haven't seen before." She looked at the doc and giggled. "Right, Dr. Baad?"

I didn't have the heart to inform dear Gertrude that, in fact, I had never seen a butt like that before, and I was a little freaked out by its close proximity.

"I have to go to the ladies' room," I said, and quickly slipped through the door before Mrs. Noodle had a chance to object. When I closed the door, I leaned against it, fanning my face.

"Are you all right?" asked a passing nurse. "You look very flushed."

"I'm fine," I answered. "Just a hot flash." And I hurried off to the bathroom before Gertrude heard my voice and called me back in. In the restroom, I splashed cold water on my face, put the toilet seat down, and sat on it while taking some deep breaths. If this was an example of doctor's office experiences with the Noodles, I might have to limit my function to strictly dropping off and picking up. Accompanying a client inside was just too close, literally, for comfort.

Finally, I went back to the room and was glad to see that Gertrude had once again covered herself.

"What took you so long, Jill? There was a lot for you to write down. The doc here said that I have a big hemorrhoid. That's what the lump is. Doctor Baad, can you repeat everything so my driver can write it down?"

I was beginning to think that Dr. Baad really wasn't so bad after all. He had the patience of a saint with Gertrude, and even took the time to reiterate to me everything that he had told her in my absence. Baad was good!

With the exception of a prescription for hemorrhoid cream, Mrs. Noodle, like her husband, was also given a clean bill of health. It made me wonder, though. I hoped the good doctor wasn't just trying to keep them away for another year—not that I would blame him. I looked at the car clock. Eleven-thirty. Nice and early, with plenty of afternoon time for me!

"Jill," said Gertrude as she situated her fully clothed (thank heavens!) body next to me, "since we're already out for the day, would you mind taking me on a few errands? I'll pay you, of course."

Well, there went my free afternoon. I was one of those people who had a hard time saying no to people, so I was stuck with the Noodles for longer than anticipated.

"I have an even better idea," she continued, "Why don't we stop for lunch first? It's time for Ed and me to eat, and Ed likes those ninety-nine cent burgers at Burger

King. Actually, Ed likes anything that costs only ninety-nine cents!" Gertrude laughed and whispered to me, "He's a bit of a cheapskate, Jill, but don't tell him I said so."

I could feel my alone time swiftly diminishing as I pulled into the first Burger King that we came across.

"It's our treat, Jill," said Gertrude as we found a table. "What do you want? We'll get it so you can hold the table. I like this one by the window. We always try to sit here when we come."

I looked around at the other ten empty tables, five of them by windows, but said only, "I'll just have a diet soda and a side salad, please."

"No wonder you're so skinny, Jill. You eat like a rabbit. And diet soda is no good for you. It gives you cancer. I'll get you a regular soda."

"No, Mrs. Noodle. Diet, please. I don't drink it that often, so don't worry, OK?"

She walked up to the line, not looking pleased with my request, so I figured I'd better keep an eye on her just in case she tried to sneak in the regular soda. When it was their turn to order, it looked like the Noodles were arguing. I was tempted to go over by them, but I didn't want to upset her if we lost our table, so I stayed in my seat.

I needn't have worried. They were still fighting when they got back to the table, and loudly too.

"I don't understand why you couldn't get the ninety-nine cent burger like I did! Why do you have to have the fancy stuff? My burger's not good enough for you, Gertie?" grumbled an angry-faced Mr. Noodle.

"I already told you," answered Mrs. Noodle in a subdued voice. "I'm not in the mood for a hamburger, plus I like their fish fillet sandwiches. Why can't you just let it go?"

"Because you had to have the $2.99 sandwich! That's why! You always want the best!"

"Fine," said a now crying Gertie. "I don't want it anymore!" And with that, she got up, threw her $2.99 fish sandwich in the garbage, and stalked out the door.

I watched Mrs. Noodle march over to the car. I didn't know what to do. Mr. Noodle was chomping on his burger, but I had definitely lost my appetite.

"I think I'll eat my salad when I get home. I'm really not hungry just yet," I said as I arose and hurried away before he could stop me. "I'll just open the car for Gertrude, and we'll wait for you."

"Hmph" was all he muttered, his mouth full.

"I told you he was cheap!" she exclaimed when I got outside. "That's OK, though! I'll get him back! Just wait till dinner! We'll see how he feels when I throw a can of SpaghettiOs in front of him! And that's it! Just the can...unopened! I'll teach him not to mess with me!"

We sat there and waited for Ed, and I started freaking out a little. I thought about my own husband, who was also a tad frugal. Would this be us in another twenty-five years? Fighting over burgers versus fish fillets? I certainly hoped not!

Gertrude was very upset, so she informed me that the afternoon errands were off and asked me to take her and *him* home. The car was so quiet that you could hear a pin drop, and when I glanced in the rearview mirror, I saw that Ed had a meek expression on his face. All of his blustering was apparently over.

As soon as I pulled up to their house, Mr. Noodle jumped out of the car and hurried around to his wife's door to open it for her. When she got out, he pulled a Burger King sack from behind his back and said, "Please forgive me, Gertie, for being a jerk. I love you! And look, I went back and got you another fish fillet! I even got you fries, too!"

"You *are* a big jerk," his wife said, "but I forgive you! Sometimes I really don't think you can help it. Must be one of those genetic things. Your father was a cheapskate, too! Next time, I'll just get the 99-cent burger."

The Noodles bid me goodbye and walked arm and arm up the stairs to their home. I watched them for a minute and once again compared them to my husband and me. I supposed that everyone had faults. I spent and Vic saved, just like Gertie and Ed. It was like a marital balancing act. Then I laughed to myself, thinking that I didn't eat Burger King anyway!

CHAPTER 26—CRONIES AT CRONY'S

The end of March marked the conclusion of the long, cold, wet winter. The sun was getting brighter and the days longer. But most importantly, The Forever 39ers were getting antsy to do something fun! Besides work and exercise, I didn't think that any of us had gotten out much in the last three months. Kate's fifty-first birthday was a month ago, and we had yet to celebrate it as a four-some.

We decided that a Friday night visit to our favorite local bar/restaurant, Crony's, was in order. Kate, Barb, Patty, and I had been going there since we were in our twenties, and it appeared as if the rest of the patrons had been doing the same thing. Friday nights drew the "younger" crowd, meaning those fifty and over. On Saturdays, the establishment was home to a more mature group, pretty much meaning anyone eligible for Social Security.

Since, with the exception of Patty, we were all married, the age of the crowd had no impact on us. Even Patty wasn't searching for her Mr. Right at Crony's! For us, the place was close, drew good bands, sold cheap alcohol, and had no cover charge. Oh, and we had a lot of laughs there. But then again, one can't put a price on laughter!

Much of our entertainment stemmed from the other people who frequented Crony's. We had nicknames for our favorite regulars. "Cotton Top" was a seventy-ish man with a hairstyle that was a perfect cotton ball. "The Widower" was a friendly-looking elderly man who always seemed to be having a good time and, for whatever reason, struck us as a widower. He constantly had a smile on his face and looked too nice for someone to have divorced him. There was "the Big Girl," who, though she was overweight, had earned her name by having the loudest/biggest voice in the place, not an easy task in an already earsplitting environment. "Ms. Hook-Up" (and I use the "Ms." title loosely) was an amazon of a woman with close-cropped blond hair, super-short dresses, spiked heels, and always a guy locked to her lips by the end of the evening. (She scared us a little.) There was a petite, overly made-up sixty-ish woman who dressed like a twenty-year-old. We dubbed her "the Cute Lady," simply because I had spoken to her one night and thought her to be sweet and nice. Last, but certainly not least, was "Big Butt." She was a fifty-something-year-old, normal-appearing woman who generally wouldn't warrant a nickname. But Big Butt had earned the title from the overactive, overzealous, and immodest use of her derrière. It was big, round, prominent, and usually clad in very tight jeans. Its owner shook it at the patrons and the musicians nonstop while either boogying or, in some cases, pole dancing. She gave new meaning to the word "flaunt"!

Don't get me wrong: we weren't so vain as to think that we couldn't be given nicknames too. Still, we weren't weekly regulars, and all in all we were a relatively toned-down group. We went if we had a free Friday or Saturday, or if, as was the case tonight, there was a particular band that we wanted to see and an occasion to celebrate.

Another benefit of Crony's was that we didn't have to get all decked out to go there. The customers' attire ranged from shorts (jeans in the cooler months) and sneakers to little black dresses. Most of the men wore either button-down shirts or three-button polos with khakis. The women wore anything and everything. We usually showed up in jeans and pretty tops, with attractive Patty being the best dressed out of the four of us. Barb tended to be the most dressed down, sometimes arriving in sneakers, as her feet were heel-shod all day at work. Kate and I fell somewhere in between, and sometimes, unplanned, we would arrive in similar ensembles.

We'd had the foresight to reserve one of the tables by the dance floor. This way, we would be comfortable throughout the evening and would be able to keep an eye on our bags if we danced. Many times we came early to eat, so by the time the band began playing, we were ready to dance off the calories. We tended to eat extra on these outings and not feel guilty because we knew that aerobic exercise would follow our massive food consumption. Maybe it was just a great excuse to overeat, but it worked for us!

The band came on at ten, and by ten-thirty, as I made a bathroom run, I noticed that all of the regulars seemed to be here, ready and raring. I headed back to the table, but the dance floor was packed and I had to wait until the song was over before I could reach my friends. Within minutes, which was the norm for Crony's, a man about my age magically appeared at my side. It always amazed me how these guys showed up out of nowhere! Did they hide under tables or in dark corners, waiting for the first sight of an unaccompanied female, or did they secretly stalk the women until they could get them alone? It wasn't as if they were creepy guys; they were more on the annoying side and sometimes reeked of desperation. I felt a little sorry for them, but not sorry enough to chat or dance with them.

"Hi!" Blue Shirt yelled in my ear. "Are you here by yourself?"

"I'm with friends," I also yelled while pointing in the general direction of the girls.

"Do you come here often?" he continued.

Really? Did he seriously just ask me that? What a loser! I kept my eyes glued to the dance floor, waiting for the song to come to an end. Also, I didn't want to look Blue Shirt in the eyes lest he think I was remotely interested in him. It didn't take much for the men in this place to misinterpret a woman's friendliness. Heaven forbid that a female make eye contact!

"Sometimes," I answered. "Usually to see a certain band. Like this one."

"I'm kind of new to this scene. Separated six months now," he informed me, as if I cared.

"Well, good luck with that," I said as the music came to a break between songs. I scooted back over to my table before he could utter another word and threw myself into the booth with a feigned forehead-sweat wipe.

"Ouch," exclaimed Kate. "What's your problem? You almost squished me to death!"

"Sorry. I was running for my married life! Is he coming?"

"Is *who* coming?" asked Barb from across the table. "What took you so long anyway?"

"The guy in the blue shirt." I looked around. "Never mind. I think I lost him."

"Was he cute?" asked Patty. "Or I suppose I should ask, was he our age or younger?"

"Our age," I said, "but I thought you were off men for now? Is that stage over already?"

"Oh right! I forgot for a minute," she replied. "I'm still off men. Eventually, I'll probably take them up again though!"

"Is that him?" whispered Kate, as yes, indeed, Blue Shirt sauntered past our table. "He was checking you out!"

I laughed. "He'll just have to find some other lucky girl to flirt with. There's always Big Butt! She's already grinding away!"

"I saw her while you were in the bathroom," said

Barb. "Do you think she wakes up sore the next morning from contorting her body that way? I mean, I get sore just bending over to tie my sneakers!"

Kate added, "I get sore from sex! That's why I try to limit it to once a month!"

"Good one, Kate," I smiled at her. "So who's ready to work off the pounds?" No one responded. They jumped to their feet and were on the dance floor the second I finished the question. After all, we weren't out tonight to talk. We did enough of that at Starbucks. We were at Crony's to eat, drink, and dance, in that order!

An hour later, when the band took a break, we stumbled over to our table and collapsed, huffing and puffing. I downed my white wine spritzer, then snatched Kate's and downed hers too! She was in the ladies' room, so I hoped she wouldn't notice when she returned.

"We need another round," said Patty. "I'll go get it. I'll grab Kate on the way so she can help me carry them back."

As Barb and I waited, Barb said, "Look at Kate and Patty! Are those two guys hitting on them? They look like they're twenty-five years old! What the heck!"

I turned toward the bar, and sure enough, Kate and Patty were conversing with two young guys. Holy cow! And Kate was patting the one guy's shoulder. She looked like she was burping him! At that thought, I began laughing uncontrollably, and after spitting my thought out to Barb, so did she! The tears were streaming down both our faces.

"What are you two laughing about?" asked Kate when they returned. "Did I miss something good?"

"Looks like we're the ones who missed the action," said Barb, still laughing. "Why were you patting that guy, Kate?"

"He was so sweet," she answered. "He tapped Patty on the shoulder and said, 'What's a beautiful woman doing buying her own drink?' Then Patty thanked him for the compliment but told him he was a tad too young for her. He looked so dejected that I patted him on the shoulder and told him that he was very cute and was bound to find a girl more his own age. Then I said that he probably wouldn't find her in Crony's, and that he and his buddies might want to go to a different club." She paused to take a sip of her drink. "They were nice-looking guys. Too bad they were so young. I might have considered once-a-week sex with one of them!"

"Kate! For someone who has so little sex and claims to like it that way, you sure do talk about it a lot," observed Barb.

"Nah. I'm just joking," replied Kate. "I'm not vaginally rejuvenated like you are!" Kate pulled her face up and out like she was tightening it, and we rolled with laughter. Then she pursed her lips, and we roared! Patty was snorting so loud that if those young guys hadn't already left, they were making a beeline for the exit now! "Girls, look! It's Blue Shirt again! How many times does that make?"

"Too many," I said. "Let's hit the dance floor before he decides to approach me again!"

The rest of the night was more of the same: lots of laughing, dancing, and general silliness. Barb and Kate got drunk and, as usual, Patty, being the designated driver, remained sober. At one point, an inebriated Kate grabbed the microphone and made a very public announcement that it was her birthday and that she was thirty-nine and holding! This earned her a "Happy Birthday" serenade from the crowd and free drink offers from everyone in the room. Needless to say, none of us paid for a single drink after that.

We closed the place down with the rest of the regulars, and as we walked to our cars, people were still shouting out "Happy Birthday!" We passed Ms. Hook-Up in her typical end-of-the-night lip-locked position. I watched her in a passionate embrace and, not for the first time, wondered what men saw in her. Maybe they kept their eyes closed. Up ahead, Big Butt staggered solo to her car. The Widower watched her with his ever-present smile, then ran to catch her arm as her heel got stuck and she did a wobble/almost-topple. The Big Girl and the Cute Lady looked to be escorting Cotton Top to his car, and he was grinning ear-to-ear. I wondered if this was their usual end-of-the-evening tête-à-tête. Good for them if it was!

I realized when I drove the short distance home that, like Starbucks, Crony's was our comfort zone. It might not be the most happening place, but it was safe and familiar. Besides, the four of us were easily amused no matter where we went. As Patty liked to say, "We could have fun in a box!"

CHAPTER 27—ANOTHER FAMILY HOLIDAY

Wow! This holiday stuff sure is a lot of work, I thought to myself as I smelled the wonderful aroma of ham and lamb coming from my oven. I had never cooked either before, nor was I cooking them now. Actually, there were many things I had never had the displeasure of cooking. Simply put, I didn't like food preparation. Apart from the occasional baking. I preferred to think of myself as more of an eater.

My mother and mother-in-law were the ones who usually did the holiday feasts, but I had volunteered my services this year. When I discovered just how daunting and overwhelming holiday entertaining was, I did the only thing that I could think of: I called my sister-in-law,

Gabby, and pleaded for assistance. Gabby was a goddess in the kitchen and also very controlling, so I knew that if I made enough "unintended" mistakes, she'd kick me out and take over. She didn't disappoint me, either. I was now in charge of table setting, food carrying, and wine drinking.

"Is there anything else I can do to help you?" I asked her.

"Not until the meat is done," she replied while whipping potatoes from scratch. "Just sit there and enjoy your wine." That was my sister-in-law, always looking out for my welfare.

I was impressed with the potatoes! Hadn't she ever heard of instant? I laughed to myself. That would be the day, when Gabby cooked *anything* out of a box! Or frozen! She'd go hungry before eating anything that came out of a freezer. I seriously doubted that she knew what a SpaghettiO or a Beefaroni was. I had hidden the offensive cans before she came lest her opinion of my cooking sink to an all-time low.

My family and Vic's were celebrating Easter at our house. To my dismay, every single one of them could make it. I already foresaw loudness and chaos, all originating from my side of the family. Mama, Papa, Pete, and Jason were relatively quiet. Gabby was the loudest of the five, but then again, like me, she also came from an over-exuberant family. As if they had read my mind, the guests began arriving, and from the noise level that filtered in from outside, it sounded like my relations.

"Mama and Papa Castillo, how the hell are you?" yelled Anthony, and I cringed. My very proper in-laws never used curse words, not even a mild one like "hell." I was probably in trouble with Mama now, as she'd blame me for Ant's profanity.

In walked the elder Castillos, accompanied by my kerchief-clad mother, my father, and my brother. Mama, true to form, was scowling, but Papa and Anthony appeared to be having an animated Mets-versus-Yankees conversation. Even though I had told both mothers to bring only dessert, they arrived with food as well. I knew this was going to anger Gabby because she had emphatically refused their offer of side dishes. To top it all off, my mother-in-law had brought mashed potatoes!

I tried to get my husband's attention, "Vic. Vic!" Finally, he approached me. "Hurry! Grab the food and hide it! Gabby will have a conniption!" I envisioned the hot-headed Spanish woman dumping food over the older women's heads. At least the kerchief and winter coat would protect my mother. I did a double take. It was fifty degrees out, and Mom had on a puffy coat! Was she kidding me? Normally, I'd say something, but I didn't want to begin the festivities with a fight. Vic and I wrestled the offending dishes from two pairs of reluctant hands and quickly brought the food downstairs to the basement.

"I don't think this is going to work," I whispered to my husband. "I think they're going to notice, don't you?"

"So, what do you suggest?" he answered, looking around for a place to put the unwanted Pyrex dishes. Our basement was a mess, crammed with various types of exercise equipment, tools, random junk, and Anthony's exiled inventions. (Those creations scared me a little: I half expected them to take on a life of their own, like a scene in a creepy sci-fi movie.)

"Let's just put them on the dining room table and pray she doesn't notice."

"Yeah, that'll work. Why didn't I think of that ingenious idea?" he retorted sarcastically.

"Jill! Why are you and Vic still holding the dishes? And why did you bring them down to the basement?" asked my mother from the top of the basement stairs.

"Oh, look! Kelly and Jim are here," I informed Mom while heading through the dining room, depositing the bowls on the table, and greeting my sister and her family in the foyer. I'd learned over the years that the best way to handle her unwanted questions was to avoid them.

"Wow! Kelly! You didn't have to get so dressed up. It's only my house," I said, hugging my sister.

"Actually, we got dressed up for church. And the children like wearing Easter outfits."

I looked at my smiling thirteen-year-old niece and eleven-year-old nephew sporting their matching holiday finest. Kelly was right; they definitely appeared to be happy in their uncomfortable-looking, but proper, clothes. Jimmy Jr. had on a suit, and Amanda was wearing a dress. Maybe I was a tad jealous. By the young age of five, Neil had already begun to balk at what he referred to as "fancy" clothes. His idea of dressing up was donning a pair of jeans, a polo shirt and his customary black sneakers.

In the kitchen, Mama Castillo attempted to assist Gabby, who tried to fend her off with denials of needing help. I knew my mother-in-law, though, and she was a persistent woman. My own mother was already seated at the dining room table by herself. I couldn't be sure if she was hungry or guarding the food. The guys had taken over the adjoining living room to watch whatever sports event was showing today.

Aunt Marie and Uncle Al arrived, and the party guests were complete. Unlike the moms, my aunt had heeded my request and brought only dessert.

I heard my dad's voice. "Gloria! Why are you sitting all by yourself?"

"I'm hungry, Tony! Didn't our daughter say three o'clock? Well, it's almost three-thirty! I suppose I should have eaten a snack before I came, but how was I to know dinner would be late?"

I looked imploringly at my aunt for help. My uncle kissed me hello, then plopped himself down with the rest of the men. Kelly was talking to Gabby, so there was no help there.

"Aunt Marie! Please!" One of her most endearing qualities, in my opinion, was that she could never say no to me. Times like this, I was forced to play on that weakness. I'd make it up to her at a later date. She knew what I was up to, and she gave me an unhappy look as she joined my mother.

Finally, the scrumptious-smelling food was served and everyone took their seats. The table looked more like a Thanksgiving feast than an Easter celebration. I didn't think I had ever seen so many side dishes on one table, though, granted, some were in duplicate. I purposely arranged the extras so that they were on the opposite end of the table from where Gabby was sitting. The ham and lamb were smack in the middle, also obscuring her view.

I added a tall, flower-filled vase for good measure.

For the next hour, people ate lavishly and uttered compliments of "yum" and "really good," and my sister-in-law preened. I had to admit that the meal was a masterpiece, one I could never have created on my own. Even Mom looked content. Mama Castillo kept inspecting her forkfuls for any flaws, but thus far seemed not to have discovered any.

Uncle Al and Vic discussed the pros and cons of the golf GPS I had given Vic for Christmas. Uncle Al thought it to be an expensive, unnecessary little gadget that probably wouldn't work as described. Vic and Pete, who also owned one, extolled its virtues. Anthony joined in the conversation and inspected the gadget. I could see the envy in his eyes, and knew that he wished he had invented a golf GPS. (No doubt, the little gizmo was going to set into motion more of his wild and creative thoughts.) He asked Vic if he could borrow it for a few days to "inspect it," and my husband grabbed it back and said, "No." Undoubtedly, Ant would have taken it apart to study its mechanics and would never have been able to reassemble it properly.

My well-behaved niece and nephew sat quietly, although Neil and Jason attempted to include Jim Jr. in a baseball conversation. Kelly and "Big" Jim talked to Mom. God bless my sister for her patience with our mother. I never could understand how the two of them managed to have civil conversations, while a few sentences with our mother had me banging my head against a wall. Unlike Ant and me, Kelly was mild-mannered and not easily exasperated. But then again, I thought that

Mom was nicer to her than to me. I swore that my mother purposely tried to incense me.

"Is it my imagination, or are there extra bowls on this table?" Gabby's thunderous voice interrupted my observations of the family. Her eyes were slits, her hands were clenched, and she reminded me of a feral black cat about to pounce.

I soothed her. "Just let it go, Gab. They meant no harm. They wanted to feel needed. It'll be more leftovers to go around."

"Uh-huh," she muttered, but thankfully, she seemed to visibly relax.

I continued, "Besides, do you really want to get on Mama's bad side? You know how long she can hold grudges!"

Finally, the always slow Papa was finished eating, and the table could be cleared. This time I told Gabby to sit and relax with her wine while the rest of us cleaned up and loaded the dishwasher.

I hadn't paid any attention to the desserts that were brought, as my mind had been focused on the food. Now, I saw that both mothers had brought the exact same dessert items: two strawberry shortcakes and two Italian cheesecakes. What were the chances? Since there was nothing I could do about it, again I placed the duplicate dishes on opposite ends of the table.

Unfortunately, nothing got past my mother or mother-in-law. I could see Mama's eyes going back and forth between the four desserts while Mom's unblinking stare settled on her female competition.

"What this?" hissed Mama. "Dos de lo mismo? You

bring lo mismo?" She glared at my mother while pointing to the almost identical confections.

Mom glared back from the other side of the table. "How was I supposed to know what you were bringing? Maybe next time you should call me and ask! Actually, this is my daughter's fault for not coordinating the desserts!" Now both women glowered at me.

Out of the corner of my eye, I saw Vic, Pete, Neil, and Jason smirking. Aunt Marie was nowhere to be seen; she was probably in a corner laughing too. Papa sat there, fork in hand, waiting for another round of extended eating. I heard Gabby and Kelly talking in the kitchen. And where the *hell* was my father?

And then a booming voice: "Mom! Mama Castillo! Relax. Look! They're not exactly the same." My brother opened one cheesecake box and picked off the orange slices, then opened one shortcake box and removed the strawberries. "See! They're all different now. Wait! One second." He ran to the kitchen and returned with a platter of fruit. He threw pineapples on the now naked cheesecake and blueberries on the no-more-strawberries shortcake, and exclaimed, "Voilà!"

While everyone except the two mothers clapped at Ant's inventive rescue, Mama gave me one final malevolent look and then turned her back to me, while Mom shook her head with a "tsk-tsk" gesture to ensure that I knew she was not happy. *So what else was new?*

Thank heavens the rest of the day was uneventful, and by the time the guests departed, everyone appeared to be satiated and content.

I heaved a sigh of relief and collapsed on the living

room couch when the last of the good-byes were said. Vic locked up and turned off the outside lights, then sat down next to me and gave me a big hug.

"You did well. It was a great Easter!"

"Thanks!" I kissed him. "But I was thinking. How would you feel about moving across the country?"

"Forget about it. They'd only follow us! I mean, who would they have to pick on if you left?"

"Very funny, but yeah, I guess you're right. It was a good idea, though!" I sighed for the second time and then yawned. "I'm going up to bed."

"Night, Jill! I love you," he called out to me.

As I walked past the still-open living room window, I swore that I glimpsed glittering, raging eyes looking fiercely at me from between the curtains of the house across the lawn. I blinked, and they were gone. And...I sighed for the third time.

CHAPTER 28—HOME ALREADY?

Wow! Was it the middle of May already? *Wasn't it just yesterday that Neil had left for college, and I had bawled my eyes out?* No way was it eight months ago! It couldn't be. I counted on my fingers. Yup! Eight months all right.

Vic drove from work to pick our son up from school and bring him home for his extremely long summer vacation. I had mixed feelings about Neil's upcoming arrival. Three months, three weeks, and one day (but who's counting?) seemed like a long time. Admittedly, I had been depressed back in the fall, as any caring mother would have been when her child was leaving home. But I had acclimated since then. The house stayed cleaner and neater. The laundry loads were considerably smaller. The food shopping bills didn't send Vic into twitch mode, and cooking was minimal. It wasn't that I didn't still miss him; it was just a different kind of missing him.

For eighteen years, I'd put my heart and soul into raising my son, and I wouldn't have traded that experience for anything in the world. With Neil's absence came the discovery that there was actually time for me now, something I had lacked for quite a while. For the last eight months, I had gotten used to a less structured life and the ability to embrace spontaneity if desired. Now, for the next almost four months, I would have to readjust my schedule to once again accommodate my son's wants and needs. At least Neil was a fairly undemanding person. Maybe I was acting a little selfish—but then again, maybe not.

When father and son walked in the door, I didn't know whether to laugh or cry! I was thrilled to see my son, of course. I was not so thrilled to see the loads and loads of personal possessions that he had brought with him. He and Vic seemed to be making endless trips back and forth to the SUV while the pile (and my eyeballs) grew to mountainous proportions.

"Where the heck did this *stuff* come from?" I moaned. "Is this all yours, or did you bring home the entire dorm's belongings?"

"I don't know, Mom. It *is* a lot! We almost couldn't fit it in the RAV4!"

"And what's with all that laundry? I thought you were keeping up with it!"

"I was! That's a week's worth plus the towels and bed stuff," he defended himself.

"One week? I don't think so! Hmph!" Then, before I

stomped off, I added, "It'll take me all summer to do your laundry and organize your things! You'll be helping me!"

"Uh, OK," he answered meekly.

When I caught a glimpse of his face, I got the guilties. The kid had just walked in the door, and I was already harping on him. That wasn't very nice of me, so I went over and gave him a hug and kiss.

"Sorry," I said. "I got a little overwhelmed, but I'm over it," I lied. It really did feel good to have him home, for now at least. He had grown up a lot in the last few months. His face was taking on a more manly appearance, enhanced by the addition of a beard. His conversational skills had undergone a drastic change. He wasn't the moody teenager anymore, so our chats and discussions were pleasurable. Although Neil would always be my baby, he certainly wasn't a baby anymore to anyone but me.

I supposed I should relish my moments with him and not complain about my motherly duties. It would only be a matter of time before he met the "perfect" woman, who would make sure that "Mommy dearest" was out of the picture.

My concern had been that Neil would meet a girl at college who lived in a different state. He'd marry her and then move far away, leaving poor Mom back in New Jersey. Well, I already had a newsflash for the yet unknown son-stealer: this mother would *not* be left behind! I would pack up and move to whatever state or country my *hijacked* son resided in!

My biggest problem would not be following Neil, but rather leaving the in-laws behind. I had visions of Vic and me stealthily loading the car in the black of the night. I could also envision Mama and Papa Castillo ready and waiting, also in the dead of the night. Then Vic would have to attempt to drive like the devil was on our butts in an attempt to outrun his dad. This could become a problem, since Papa was a tailgater and might be difficult to outmaneuver.

"Mom! Why are you frowning and making funny faces?" asked my son, who was already scanning the refrigerator for something to eat.

"I was just thinking about your Abuela and Abuelo."

He nodded his head as if my response made perfect sense. He then proceeded to make a huge hoagie using every variety of cold-cut meat and cheese that the fridge contained until the food disappeared before my disbelieving eyes. I sighed as I updated my shopping list with "large quantities of cold cuts and cheeses." Ah, the eating had begun!

"Stop twitching! You have all summer to worry about this stuff," said my husband after the last load had been brought in.

Easy for him to say! It wasn't Vic who had to worry about it! I couldn't spend months looking at this clutter. That's how I was, and he knew it, too. I was tempted to tackle it now, but I resisted.

The following morning, after taking the Noodles and Mrs. Funnier to the bank, I mentally steeled myself for the tasks ahead. While Neil was still asleep, I separated the laundry, got the first load started, and began the undesirable task of weeding through the boxes and bags of things. By "things," I meant food (there were easily twen-

ty-five chip bags), room accessories, student/desk para-
phernalia, and medicines. Some of the food was open,
and some of it was expired. It brought to mind the time
Gabby had given Neil cupcakes to bring to college. It
must have been around his birthday in October. He
brought the plastic storage container home during winter
break, unwashed and with the cupcake remains permanently stuck to the bottom and sides. *Gross!* It had taken
a full day of soaking and resoaking before I was able to
see the clear plastic of the container again. Needless to
say, my son was a bit of a pig sometimes.

"Good morning," I sing-songed to him as he sleepily
trudged into the kitchen at two o'clock in the afternoon.

He mumbled something back to me that might have
been "Good morning" but just as easily could have been a
grunt. He plodded to his den and sat in his chaise lounge,
where I was sure he'd hang out for the remainder of the
day. Life was good when you were Neil!

For the next two days, I washed, dried, folded, and
put away laundry. I made numerous trips to the attic to
store the items he wouldn't be using again until September. I carried a lamp, a wastebasket, storage drawers, pillows, a printer, and lawn bags of bedding while my son
either slept or lounged.

On the upside, everything was washed and put away.
On the downside, though, every time I passed Neil's
room, I got resentful and annoyed. I knew he'd had a
tough year of schoolwork as a chemical engineering ma-
jor. But it still irritated me that I was doing all the work
while he watched TV and played video games. "What's
your problem?" asked Neil as I passed his den for the

twenty-seventh time that day. *But who's counting?*

"Nothing!" I grunted.

"OK," he said, and resumed his gaming and television viewing.

Neil had two televisions, one for watching twenty-four hours of sports and one for Xbox playing. His laptop was used for online gaming.

I stopped in his doorway. "I've given you the weekend off, but tomorrow I want you to start looking for a job. You can't spend your summer sleeping late and then doing this all day." I waved my hand at him, his chair, and his electronics.

"A job! Already? I just got home! I need a break!"

"You've had a break for eighteen and a half years, and that break is o-v-e-r! We gave you a car for free, but you need your own money for gas. We're not paying for it or your takeout food anymore, either. I didn't say that you need to work your butt off. Just a part-time job is fine."

"Uh-huh," he answered with that "How annoying is she?" look on his face.

The next morning, true to my word, I e-mailed him links to employment sites, woke him up at a decent hour, and sent him off in his "free" car to look for a job.

He hated me. I knew it. But that came with the parent territory, and I was used to it.

Moms seemed to bear the brunt of their child's animosity, while dads, for the most part, got to be the good guys. When Neil was a toddler, I was the one who used the no word, every day, all day. Vic would come home, and it would be playtime with fun Daddy. Then, for thirteen years, I was the homework nag, tutor, and tester. I especially enjoyed the grammar school years, when schoolwork culminated in Neil throwing a tantrum and me screaming in frustration, then both of us crying. When Dad came home, the work was done and the son was happy again, just in time to bond with his father. They'd watch sports on TV or maybe just throw a ball around. Good times!

When Neil turned sixteen, the serious stuff began and made the toddler years seem like they'd been a piece of cake. Forget teaching him how to walk! Now I (a stupid "girl") had to teach a hormonal, moody teen boy how to drive. Ugh! Now *those* were fights! They'd end in Neil stomping into the house, hating my guts, while I headed straight for the wine. No glass! I drank right from the bottle!

The dreaded day came when he got his license. I prayed every time he left the house until he was safely back home. I'd tell him to text me whenever he was going to be on the road and again when he got to his destination so I'd know he was OK. Needless to say, he'd forget, then not check his cell phone for my repeated frantic texts. One time, I was so worried that I sent Vic out on the highway in search of our son, who was not answering his cell phone. It turned out that Neil was fine and had forgotten to call me. I know I had a mini-heart attack that day. Like I said, good times!

I had calmed down somewhat in the last year and a half with the driving anxiety, but I still worried when he was out and didn't relax until he was safely home. I supposed there were certain things that moms fretted about forever. I didn't even want to think about how much I'd worry when he moved out for good. One day at a time for me.

Right now, my main concern was my dear son's need to obtain a job. He had never worked before, much to my dismay. Last summer, I'd been on his case for a month to find something, but he hadn't, mostly due to lack of trying. As July came to an end, I'd given up because school was going to begin in three weeks. But this year I was determined that Neil find employment. I intended on berating him every day, and today was day one of what I was sure he'd consider another form of mom torture.

Neil was back home an hour later.

"What did you forget?" I asked, surprised by his early appearance.

"Nothing. I'm done."

"Excuse me," I said to his retreating back. "You weren't even gone long enough to get gas! Seriously, why are you home already?"

"I'm done. I swear! Every place told me that I have to fill out an application online, so I gave up. I'll just stay home and fill out apps."

I didn't know what to say. Neil was a college kid looking for a short-term summer job, and he had no previous work experience. I was dumbfounded. I believed him, but I felt frustrated. Applying online was so impersonal and seemed like an impossible way to obtain employment.

I was already developing a feeling of foreboding. Visions of my son having a grand old time while relaxing all summer long in his comfy black chair danced through my head. I looked at the wall clock. One o'clock. Late enough! I walked over to the fridge, grabbed the wine bottle, and drank!

CHAPTER 29—"UNSUITABLE" DECISIONS

Kate, Patty, Barb, and I rode solemnly in my car early one Saturday morning on our way to a terrible destination. No one spoke a single word, but our expressions spoke volumes. We were not happy campers. Today was the once-a-year dreaded day, a day we would happily have given up had age, gravity, and style changes not forced us to repeat it annually. We were on our way to the mall to go *bathing suit* shopping! I didn't dare say the words aloud for fear of causing tears.

I thought that most women, either after childbirth or once they hit their thirties, began to suffer from dread and fear (yes, fear) of shopping for a swimsuit. There were also those of us who hated it from the time we were in our teens. It was probably on some top ten list of "Why It's So Difficult to Be a Woman." It was also another one of those "female things" that men totally didn't get. Why should they? Bathing trunks were just a water-friendly version of shorts. If only it was that simple for us girls!

"You'd better give it a little more gas, Jill. Even the old people are giving us the finger!"

"Sorry, Patty. I was daydreaming." I left out the source of my musings. It was still too early to voice the words, and we were only on our first cup of coffee. We'd have our second at the mall in the hope that we'd be fortified to face the day ahead.

An hour later, we dragged our feet through the department store en route to our destination. When we arrived, we stopped and stared at the huge assortment of swimwear. There were two reasons behind our hesitation. First, as always, we were overwhelmed. Second, we needed a quick assessment of the "in" styles before we began the hunt. The whole process would take us hours, and because it was a lot of work, we'd take a quick caffeine break to revive our weary bodies and minds. We wouldn't dare eat for fear of extra stomach bloat! The goal was to purchase at least one suit by day's end. The girl who didn't would go home deeply depressed and feeling like a failure. Going together helped us achieve our goal.

"Looks like animal prints are still going strong," said Barb miserably. "Why can't these designers realize that large-bottomed women *do not* look appealing in them? We look like the animals that we're wearing! Actually, some animal behinds are smaller than mine!"

Under normal circumstances, Barb's comment would have elicited at least a giggle from us, but this was no laughing matter! We each had our specific likes and dislikes, and we knew which styles would look horrible on us. Unfortunately for Barb, animal prints had been stylish for a while now and didn't appear to be ending any time soon.

"Thank God for dark-colored one-pieces," she continued as she approached the section containing them.

"I guess it's split-up time," said Patty. "We'll meet at the dressing rooms when we have our first batch narrowed down to six suits." That was all that was allowed in the room at one time.

Kate went in Barb's direction. I couldn't remember the last time I had seen her in a two-piece, unless I counted a bra and underwear. And Kate wore her underwear so high that they gave the impression of old-fashioned one-piece undergarments.

Patty and I headed toward the section containing the separates, but there our similarity ceased. Whereas Patty's slim, no-cellulite body could attractively carry off a bikini, I needed to stick with the extra-coverage bottoms. I believe they were called "full coverage." Whatever the case, I needed my entire butt and abdominal region encased, preferably with a heavy-duty, Spanx-type fabric. After deciding on bottoms, we would meet up at the tops, but still our needs would differ. Where Patty breasts still appeared to stick more out than down, mine were deflated balloons, the victims of pregnancy. She could get away with the cute little triangle, while I needed the push-up-and-in top that could stand up on its own. Then again, if I lost it in the water, it would stay buoyed long enough for me to retrieve it! What can I say? I liked to look at the bright side of life.

I picked out a swimsuit in various sizes and two patterns to start off the trying-on sessions. One (sorry, Barb) was a red-and-black cheetah print, and the other was a colorful paisley. Considering the earliness of the day, I was proud of myself for already discovering two patterns that I liked, and they both had high bottoms in solid matching colors! What were the chances? I had no problem with multicolored tops, but I drew the line when it came to my lower section. Like Barb, there was no way I was wrapping it in patterns designed for young girls with perfect little rear ends. Fifty-year-old moms simply did not give off the same sexy effect, no matter how fit we were. Well, at least in my opinion.

Patty showed up after me, carrying what appeared to be bathing suits from the children's department. I squinted, and I still couldn't make out what they looked like because they were teeny-tiny bathing suits probably in equally small sizes. Hmph! I decided it would be perfectly acceptable for me to hate my friend for the day!

Barb was next, with her typical yearly purchase: modest, solid-colored, body-shaping/body-slimming suits. There were a navy, a brown, and a black. All were similar to the ones that she already owned except that they were in a larger size.

Kate was the last to arrive, and she was holding a multitude of maillot suits in a variety of colors. She must have grabbed every color they came in, plus three sizes of each.

"What's with the colors?" I asked. "You never buy bright suits! Is that a pink I see in there? And I thought we agreed on six at a time?"

"Well," she replied a tad huffily, "I've decided to change my image. Just because I'm wide-shouldered doesn't mean that I can only wear dark colors. I can wear whatever I want, Jill! And I took a few sizes because I don't know my size anymore. I think they make these things smaller every year! What's the purpose of that? To make me feel fatter than I already feel?"

Barb, Patty, and I stared first at Kate's retreating back and then at one another. I shrugged at my friends. Ever since she'd been pregnant with Lou Jr., I couldn't recall Kate ever wearing anything other than dark one-pieces. I had no idea what had gotten into her now. Per-haps it was the stress of the day.

"So now do we have to compliment her when she walks out in that ghastly bright green number I saw on her arm?" asked Barb. "I don't want to hurt her feelings, but we're not supposed to lie about these important deci-sions. She even picked yellow! Is she nuts?"

"Hey, guys! Are you coming or what?" yelled Kate.

We got situated in our respective dressing rooms and commenced the dreaded deed. The four of us tried on our bathing suits and then emerged with the first one that fit. We came out in unison to stand in front of the large, add-ten-pounds-to-you mirror in the fluorescent-lit room. I never could understand why stores didn't put a small, make-you-look-ten-pounds thinner mirror in a low-lit ar-ea. If they couldn't do that, then they should at least pro-vide each woman with a couple of glasses of wine to soften their self-criticism.

I sighed loudly and finally opened my eyes to gaze at my half-naked body, only my gaze was immediately drawn to my friend. Yowza! What the hell was Kate wearing? I looked in the mirror at Barb and Patty's stunned faces and couldn't hold it in. I started giggling. Within seconds, my two friends joined me!

"What are you laughing at? Are you making fun of me?" said an indignant Kate.

"I'm sorry, Kate." More giggles. "But you look like a giant Sunkist orange," said Barb between guffaws.

"Oh my God! I really *do*! Stick a straw in me, and you'll have orange juice!"

That was it! The four of us sat on the floor in our bathing suits and laughed to break our hearts! The other customers were peeking out of their stalls, and I saw a few of them also laughing.

"Try the yellow one next! It has to be worse than this," exclaimed Patty.

And it was!

"Now you're something between a taxi cab and a bumblebee," snorted Patty. "Why would they put that black border on it? I feel like it's some sick man's practical joke! A woman would *never* design a suit with that color combination!"

The green brought shouts of "Brussels sprout!" "Supersized Tic Tac!" And the best one, from Barb: "If you wiggle, you'll look like Jell-O!"

With the pink came "Bazooka!" "Cotton candy!" "Miss Piggy!"

The red, lavender, and turquoise suits were no better.

Finally, Kate put on a pretty navy, one-shoulder number with white bordering the strap and neckline. It was simple yet stylish, and we all nodded our heads and exclaimed, "That's the one!" "It's perfect!" "You look so slim!"

Kate decided to get a second similar suit in black with red accents, then declared herself happily finished. One down, three more to go.

The six that Patty selected naturally all looked good on her, which made Barb, Kate, and me jealous. But being the good friends that we were, we still offered our opinions on which were the most flattering. I knew I wouldn't be sitting next to *her* on the beach, though! She chose two skimpy bikinis, one in red and the other in a zebra print, and was done. No added enhancement features for her!

Barb was the easiest. She only had to try on one of her suits, as the others she picked were exactly the same, just in different colors. It was a halter style with high-cut legs and made her top look bigger, her bottom look smaller, and her legs look longer. After some indecision, she settled on navy and brown.

I was the last to go and felt pressured because of it. We never finished this quickly. If I didn't pick out a couple, we'd be stuck here for at least another hour. I tried on the cheetah first and stared at myself in the offensive mirror. Although my body wasn't great, it wasn't horrendous either. It was pretty much the same one I'd had all my life, only older-looking. My thighs, in my opinion, were my worst feature. If only I could suck some fat from them and inject it into my boobs, I'd look so much better! I had a little tummy, but at fifty, I was fortunate that it didn't severely protrude. From what I'd heard, that feature was just around the corner though. My legs were too veiny, but I didn't have the money or the guts to have the procedures that would get rid of the unsightly marks. I had gone for a consult after I gave birth. The doctor scared the daylights out of me when she described the process, then scared me more when she named the cost.

"Jill? What's wrong? It looks cute! Don't you like it?" said Kate.

"It's fine. I was just thinking about my body and what I wish I could do to change it."

Kate got up and hugged me. "I thought we agreed when we turned fifty that there would be no more body recriminations. Remember?"

"That's right," added Barb. "We are who we are! We have to accept our attributes *and* our flaws and be happy that we're the wonderful, young-looking women that we are! This is supposed to be the beginning of our 'proud to be a woman' years!"

"And I saw your faces when I was modeling my bikinis," said Patty, "but you girls are crazy to be envious of me. You all have so much! Great families! Beautiful homes! What I'm really jealous of is that the three of you have been blessed to be able to give birth and nurture your children. That's never going to happen for me. So give me a break and let me at least have a better body than you. OK?"

We answered in the affirmative, then group-hugged. And Barb was right. I usually tried not to be so hard on myself, but bathing suit shopping can do that to a girl. I marched, head held high and stomach sucked in, back into the dressing room and finished trying the swimwear on. In the end, I chose the ones that I had originally admired: the cheetah and the paisley.

After our purchases were made and we finally exited the department store, Kate said the words that all of us were thinking: "I'm starving! How about cheeseburgers and fries, girls?"

We didn't need to hear *those* words twice! Immediately, we set off for the restaurant, laughing and trying to outrun one another. Bathing suit shopping was hard work! It was time for our reward!

CHAPTER 30—THE GREAT FALL

Vic and I would be married twenty-five years on June 14.
Yes, we had gotten married on Flag Day. On the upside,
Vic had no excuses for forgetting our anniversary. On the
downside, on the day of our wedding, there had been a
big Flag Day parade on an avenue that my already-late
limousine had to cross to get from my house to the
church. Our five o'clock nuptials turned into five-thirty
ones after I was forced to wait for smiley-faced cheer-
leaders, bands, color guards, and majorettes to march by.
Just as there was a lull in the show and the limo started
creeping forward, a large group of shuffling old VFW
men had crossed our path. On the verge of a breakdown, I
jumped out of the limo into the stifling, humid, ninety-
five-degree air with my long-sleeved, high-necked, poufy

Victorian-style gown and marched right into the center of the turtle brigade. I pointed to my gown, the limo, and the opposite side of the avenue and put my hand out like an overdressed crossing guard. The startled seniors continued to shuffle, only this time while standing in place, giving the appearance of rows of swaying cornstalks with caps on. The dense, humid air accentuated the effect. I quickly waved my car across the street and then ran in my stilettos to hop back in. To this day, I still rue our decision to cut corners and not hire a videographer. What a sight that must have been!

To celebrate our significant anniversary, we were spending Saturday night at The Ritz-Carlton in New York City. We'd begin our day at the play *War Horse,* move on to a romantic dinner at the Capital Grille, and follow that up with a leisurely stroll through Central Park. Although we had lived in New Jersey all of our lives, we had never done an overnight in the city.

I chose a pretty, flowy, peach-and-pastel-colored off-the-shoulder dress with flat silver thongs. A pair of large silver hoop earrings and a couple of thick bangle bracelets completed the ethnic effect. Even Vic was dressed nicely in black pants and a black, short-sleeved button-up shirt, although there was no ethnic look going on with his outfit.

War Horse, as anticipated, was very good. There was a lull between the play and our dinner reservations, so we took the opportunity to check into our luxurious Ritz room.

"Let's walk around the hotel before we eat," I said, "since this will probably be our first and last time here. I

can't believe how expensive it is. Ahh…to have money!"
Vic took a quick picture of me in the lobby standing in
front of a sign that said "The Ritz-Carlton." I was going
to make it my profile picture on Facebook. No one needed to know that this was my one and only visit.

After oohing and aahing (discreetly, of course), we
headed out to dinner, which was fantastic. I had to admit,
our anniversary was turning into a wonderful and memo-
rable experience.

It was a star-filled, moonlit night, and Central Park
was alive with vendors, joggers, families, and lovers, all
enjoying the beautiful evening. Vic and I strolled along
the walkway bordering the bike path, and just as I turned
to comment to Vic on the park's liveliness, my right foot
hit air instead of pavement. In my eagerness to speak, I
had unknowingly turned my body and my foot missed the
curb. I slid forward, and as I fell onto the blacktop, my
left leg twisted under me. As soon as butt hit leg, I
thought I had broken it (the leg, not the butt). The pain
was excruciating, and apparently so was my scream, as
everyone in a one-block radius came to a dead halt, including cyclists, dogs, and squirrels. For a second, as I
looked around, I thought that maybe this was some
strange dream sequence where everyone except me was
frozen in time. There was no way this was real, no way
that I could have done something *this* stupid. Wrong! As
I caught a glimpse of Vic's mouth open like the letter *O*, I
realized I wasn't asleep. And then I thought, *"He's going
to kill me!"*

"What's wrong with you? Why don't you pay attention to where you're going?" he yelled at me. I began cry-

ing, and his face softened. "Are you all right?"

I gestured for him to come closer, then whispered, "I think I broke my ankle." Indeed, it hurt like hell when I pulled my leg out from under me. It was already swelling and turning an ugly shade of purple.

As much as I didn't want to, I finally uttered the dreaded words, "I think I need to go to the hospital." And I cried even harder.

My husband lifted me from the curb and sat me on a bench. Vic had worked many years for New York Presbyterian Hospital, so he immediately pulled out his cell phone and called a good friend in a high place with many connections, to inform him of the situation and ask for advice. I watched his animated, nervous, sweating face and knew that he was both worried and mad at me.

All I kept thinking was *I can't believe I ruined our anniversary! I'm such a clumsy jerk! That's* what I was crying about, not the pain. I could deal with pain. I couldn't deal with the fact that I had upset my husband and destroyed our evening. Plus, our room had cost a pretty penny, and I'd probably feel guilty about that forever. I knew how strongly Vic felt about wasted money. Maybe I could endure the discomfort and finish off our romantic night at The Ritz. A couple of Motrin should dull the pain for a few hours. Perhaps I'd take four just to be on the safe side. Then I looked down at my now eggplant-like foot and thought better of that idea.

Vic was still going back and forth with hospital phone calls, so I elevated my leg on the bench and tried to get more comfortable. I supposed I couldn't blame him for being angry with me. I had always been a klutz. I

tended to trip, stub, bump, and fall more frequently than
the average person. I didn't watch where I was going or
lift my feet when walking, and the combination of the
two made me a danger to myself, others, and also inani-
mate objects. When I was younger, my dearly departed
grandmother described me as "a bull in a china shop" and
referred to my stride as "walking like a truck horse,"
whatever the heck that meant! Vic and Neil called me a
clumsy person made more so by carelessness. The sad
part was that I thought I *was* being careful! The more I
thought about it, the more I concluded that this probably
wasn't totally my fault. It probably could have happened
to anyone, even Vic. He'd done some funky moves in his
day too! I should probably remind him of that. Later,
though. Now might not be the perfect time.

I pulled out my cell phone, and while Vic wasn't
looking, I called Kate. I needed someone in my corner.
Besides, she would provide entertainment if we got stuck
at the hospital too long.

After I briefly whispered my mishap into the phone,
Kate exclaimed, "You did *what*?" So I had to repeat the
story for the second time, which was hard because Kate
tended to interject often.

"Kate! Forget the details for now! Can you meet us
at the hospital? Please!"

"OK, OK! I'll be there as quickly as I can!"

"Ready?" asked Vic. "We can take a cab. The ER
will be waiting for us."

An hour later, I was settled in a bed after a whirlwind
arrival. The ER Director had been waiting for us at the
door when we got there, and I was immediately taken for

X-rays while Vic filled out the necessary paperwork. I was brought back to my emergency room cubicle just as Kate walked in.

With her usual flourish, she threw her arms around me, causing the narrow gurney to roll sideways into Vic's stomach. As he struggled to catch his breath, Kate checked out my ankle and then began bawling.

"Oh, Jill! Your summer is ruined! And we just bought new bathing suits! Yours were so cute too!"

I tried giving her the "shut up" look with my eyes, but I was too late. My husband's selective hearing had caught her comment, and just as I was about to fabricate an excuse for the unneeded purchases, my guardian angel appeared in the guise of a doctor.

"Mrs. Castillo? I have some good news for you. Fortunately, you didn't break anything." He paused and waited as Kate and I high-fived. Then he cleared his throat to get our attention. "But you do have a very bad sprain."

"Thanks, Doc," I said, and jumped off the gurney. "Argh!" I screamed in pain as tears came to my eyes.

"Seriously, Jill! Are you nuts?" My husband wore the "I'm mad at her *and* she's an idiot" expression now.

"As I was saying, there are no fractures, but you tore ankle ligaments. You may not want to be jumping any time soon. I'm going to have to put a splint on your foot to immobilize it and allow healing. You'll also have to use crutches for a couple of weeks. Someone from physical therapy will come in and show you how to use them."

After the doctor put on the splint, I was given instructions to rest, elevate, and ice. My crutches arrived shortly afterward, and I studied them warily. Again, I thought of my propensity for clumsiness. This did not bode well for me or those around me. Kate and Vic must have been thinking the same thing, because they exchanged looks.

Now or never, I thought as I grabbed the crutches and assumed the crutch-walking position. According to the therapist, I was supposed to hold my bad leg in the air in front of me while hopping on the other foot, after first moving the crutches forward to a point beyond my good toes. Did he know whom he was talking to? He said that after a while I'd be able to do this fancy maneuvering without thinking about it. Kate laughed out loud at that one!

"Well, here goes nothing," I announced. Leg up and forward. Hop! Oops! Forgot the damn crutches! Falling backward! Caught!

"You might want to move the crutches first this time," said my wiseass husband.

For the next ten minutes, I practiced, and almost every time, the therapist had to catch me. This was *not* going to work out! I was not a person cut out for crutches, and I was already exhausted.

"Excuse me, Mrs. Castillo," came the voice of an approaching nurse with a walker in her hands. "You look to be having a difficult time with the crutches. Why don't you try the walker?"

Aha! At last, someone who understood me! I put my hands on both sides of the walker and hopped off as if I had practiced for years! I stopped, raised my hands in a victory gesture, and almost fell. I quickly righted myself and hopped back to Vic and Kate. Both hands on the "wheel" from now on!

"I'm ready to go! Let's blow this joint! Kate, can you drive us back to the hotel to get our car?"

Vic volunteered to get Kate's car. As soon as he was out of earshot, she whispered, "You had me worried there for a while, but I'm OK now. I think you can still keep the bathing suits."

CHAPTER 31—WALKER-ING

This was my first experience with a sprained ankle. I had never torn or broken anything before, and I was in no way prepared for the daily restrictions that being "disabled" imposed upon you. After only two days of walker-ing, I had already had enough. I felt like I was going to lose my mind and plunge into a deep depression. It took me forever to get from point A to point B, and by the time I got there, I was exhausted. I had never been one to kick up my heels (or, in my present state, sneakers) and read a book or watch television during the day when there were at least a dozen errands or chores for me to do. I canceled my chauffeuring excursions with Mrs. Funnier and the Noodles. I spent most of the time sitting in my computer chair and staring at the screen, waiting for something exciting to happen on Facebook. Go figure. My dejection prevented me from picking up a magazine or even calling anyone. My right leg was already killing me from hopping on it, and my hands hurt from holding on to the walker. To be honest, I felt sorry for myself.

I moved four of my kitchen chairs to locations throughout the first floor where I would need them. Well, actually, Neil moved them. I was sitting on one that he placed by the kitchen sink when I suddenly burst into tears.

Almost as if he'd planned it, Neil walked into the kitchen, did a double take, and asked, "What's your problem?" As cold as it sounded, I knew that his brusque question was his way of showing concern. He's a typical guy. Heaven forbid he show emotion.

"Nothing. I'm just feeling sorry for myself," I answered with an exaggerated woeful expression.

"Oh. OK." And off he went.

I didn't admit it to him, but now I was glad he was unemployed. I would need his help in the upcoming weeks. Then again, that might be the push he needed to get a job. I stopped crying and grinned evilly. Hmm. I should have sprained my ankle a month ago! An injury for a mom can be a job incentive for her child!

The doorbell rang. Who would come here on a Tuesday afternoon? "Neil! The door!" After eighteen years, one would think he'd realize you had to answer doorbells and telephones when they rang, but nope! Even Vic had an aversion to phones. He'd stare at the caller ID, yell, "It's for you," and continue along with his business. That was OK, though. Sometimes I didn't answer the door when his mother was out there (on those rare days when she forgot her key). I knew she suspected it and voiced her suspicions to her son. Payback's a bitch!

"Neil! My man! What's up? Where's my disabled sister?"

I grinned. Anthony was here! I'd have some entertainment for a while!

He walked in with a Starbucks caramel macchiato for me, a caramel Frappuccino for Neil, and a shopping bag filled with unknown, but probably interesting, stuff. I settled in with my coffee and waited for the show to begin.

"Mom says you should get a wheelchair so it's easier to get around." I shook my head, and he continued. "I told her you probably wouldn't want one, but she insisted that I relay the message, so I'm relaying it. Don't kill the messenger!" He began pulling things out of his goodie bag, and I sensed an invention in the making. "You're going to have to stay in your chair while I do this. I want to make some changes to the walker for your comfort and carrying ease."

First were two fluffy socks. He wrapped them around the handles so I had purple- and pink-striped handgrips.

Ant looked at me and winked. "And they're machine washable too." Next was a box full of new plastic bags, the kind that groceries are put in. These particular ones had smiley faces on them. "Now, this part is easy. You tie the bag to the bar under the side handle and use it as a garbage bag. When it's full, throw it out and put a fresh one on."

"I like the smiley faces."

He laughed. "I knew you'd appreciate that! And please take note that the socks are in your favorite colors."

"Yes, I noticed. Love them! Don't you have work now, though?"

"No worries, Jill. I always have time for you, and my inventions *are* work. So…moving right along."

The phone rang. "You know that has to be our dear mother. I'm tempted to ignore it, but she'll just keep calling back," I moaned as I picked up the phone.

"Yes, Mom. He's here." I rolled my eyes at my brother. "Yes. He told me what you said about the wheelchair." Ant rolled his eyes at me. "No, Mom. I don't want a wheelchair *or* a scooter." Both of us eye-rolling now. "I'm sure. Definitely sure. I have to go now. Talk later." I hung up before she could further impress upon me the benefits of maneuvering with wheels. I looked at Ant. "Do you ever wonder if someone switched our mother at our births?"

"All the time!"

During my conversation with Mom, Ant had continued to work his magic on my walker. Now there was a tray with a cup holder attached to the front bar, and a multisectioned purple tote bag strapped underneath. It was like a walker purse, and I thought it would really come in handy when I ventured outside the house. But even when I was home, it would be great. It was very difficult, damn near impossible, to carry anything in my hands while walking.

Just as I thought he was finished, Ant pulled out yet another gadget. It was a battery-operated bike light, which he also attached to the middle of the front bar right above the tray. Boy, he really had thought of everything!

"Done! Stand up and try it out."

I took hold of my new soft, comfy handles, and Anthony pulled one final item out of the bag. "I had this made just for you," he said, plopping a train conductor's cap on my head. I took it off to check it out. The hat was handicap-blue with a white stitched emblem exactly like the one displayed in a disabled person's car.

"That should get you special privileges when you're out!"

"Gee, Ant. I kinda thought hopping around on a walker with my leg in a splint would have done the same, don't you?"

"Maybe," he answered, "But how about when you're driving? How are people going to know to give you the right of way?"

"Oh. I never thought about that. Anyway, I have to say…you outdid yourself on this. It's definitely going to make my life a lot easier."

"No problem, Sis! Let me take a couple of quick pics with you in the walker and then the walker by itself. I need to bring them to my invention guy. You know…the one who reviews my stuff and lets me know if anything has future market potential. Then it's back to work for me."

"Sure, no problem." I didn't have the heart to say that his "guy" probably thought my brother was crazy. There had been many creations throughout his lifetime, and it never seemed to faze him that not a single one of them had gotten any further than his house (or mine, in certain instances, like today.) He was like an artist who spent his days doodling but never created any actual paintings that sold. But I was his sister, and I supported him no matter what. Besides, he had designed this snazzy walker for me. I put a smile on my face and did some poses, even adding a cup and food to the tray. And then he was gone, and the kitchen felt empty and depressing again.

I figured it was a good time to fill the tote with my daily essentials. I set about my task and discovered that while Ant's invention was highly functional, it was also bulky and burdensome. His intentions were good, but there was a flaw in the product, as I was rapidly discerning. Even though my hands were cushioned, they had to pick up much more weight than before with all the added gizmos. I was straining my hands and my arms and moving quite slowly in the process, and I hadn't added my own stuff yet! I hopped into the laundry room that was next to the kitchen to throw in a load of clothes, and in the process, the tray hit the doorframe and fell off.

This time Neil looked concerned when he ran to my rescue. "What the heck was that noise? Are you OK?" Then he spotted the tray on the floor and realized what had happened. "Uncle Ant's invention is already falling apart, I see. I think he overdid it this time. His attachments weigh more than the walker. You'd better be careful you don't tip over with that thing." He picked up the tray. "You're not putting this back on again!" And off he went with tray in hand. I had to admit that his protectiveness was endearing, although now I didn't have any way to carry my drinks, and I was *always* drinking one thing or another.

Oliver, who had a tendency to follow me every-where, even to the point of lying on my feet while I was going to the bathroom, was now constantly underfoot. As I hopped, he stayed within the walker area, plodding along using the space where my left leg was lifted to take his steps. We clumsily navigated as if we were in a five-legged race, and he got kicked, bumped, and pushed, fre-quently crying out more in surprise than pain. But he didn't learn and remained treading within the confines of the walker.

The next morning, I learned the hard way that there was going to be another challenge where Oliver was con-cerned. It was raining today, and whenever it was wet out, we cleaned and dried Oliver's paws after he went to do his "business." I would place myself as close to the door as possible, let Oliver in, and order him to sit/stay. But every once in a while, he would decide he didn't want to be wiped, and this morning was one of those an-noying times. Just as I precariously leaned over the front of the walker to grab his paw, he veered off. Stupidly, I leaned over the side to get to him before he tracked mud all over the house. The next thing I knew, I was on the ground and still inside the walker. My right side was ly-ing on the bar, which also meant that my good leg was trapped beneath my bad one. To add insult to injury, Oli-ver thought I was playing and jumped all over me. I shielded my head with my arms and tried to not let him hit my injured leg. I cried, "Help! Help!" No answer. Again: "Neil! Help me!" This went on for five minutes, until my leg and bathrobe were covered with paw prints.

Yuck! God only knew where those paws had been!

Finally, I heard footsteps. Neil took one look at me stuck inside the walker, on the floor, with a dog sitting atop me, and burst out laughing! Since he wasn't much of a laugh-out-loud person, I figured I must look even more ridiculous than I realized.

"Seriously? Are you going to just stand there laughing, or are you going to get me out of here?" Even as I said it, I couldn't control my own giggles.

"How do you do these things?" he finally was able to spit out as he helped me out and up, and then righted the walker. "Never mind. I'm going back to bed." Halfway up the stairs, he hesitated and turned around. "Oh, and you owe me extra sleep time today, so don't wake me up anytime soon."

For the next two weeks, I was inundated with visitors. Mama Castillo arrived promptly at six every evening with a meal in hand. Part of me thought she was being very nice, and the other part suspected that she didn't want her son and grandson to go hungry. Papa took over plant watering duty, which was fine by me except he tended to startle me when I got up in the morning. I would hop sleepily into the kitchen for my morning java, and there was my father-in-law directly outside my French doors! *Yikes!*

The first time my sister-in-law came to visit, she stopped dead in her tracks and exclaimed, "Ay yi yi! What did you do to yourself, Jill? And whatever is that thing you're using to walk? Never mind. Don't even tell me. Anthony made it for you, didn't he? He's like the Nutty Professor!" Gabby was laden with shopping bags, but unlike Mama, she had brought stuff only for me. There were several bottles of my favorite pinot grigios, a container of guacamole from Whole Foods, hunks of various cheeses, and a large loaf of French bread. She uncorked a bottle, and we spent the evening drinking, eating, and watching chick flicks. This was a perfect evening for me. Gabby would have been my ideal spouse. Besides being attentive, she knew all my likes, dislikes, and idiosyncrasies, as I did hers. We also shared a love for the *Twilight* saga, so we watched the first three movies for the *n*th time and fell asleep with contented sighs just as Bella accepted Edward's marriage proposal.

One evening, Kelly came to visit with my polyester-clad mother in tow. Apparently it was another head-to-toe day, with light blue being the color du jour. After Mom headed to the bathroom, muttering about the twenty-minute drive, I grabbed my sister by the arm and whispered, "You're on a one-hour time clock, and the clock just started ticking. Tick-tock, tick-tock."

"Jill, I still don't understand why you don't get an electric wheelchair. It would be so much easier for you to get around," said my mother as soon as she returned from the bathroom.

I could have bet my house on those being the first words out of her mouth. At least she never disappointed me in her predictability.

"For the twentieth time, *I don't want one!*" Crap! She already had me yelling. I glanced at the wall clock, took a few deep breaths, and continued. "Anyway, it's only going to be for two or three weeks. Plus, there are too many tiny steps and humps by the doorways, so it would get frustrating."

I wondered if she had heard a word I said because her only response was, "Jill! You're always yelling at me. You always were fresh. Why can't you be more like your sister? She's soft-spoken and pleasant."

I gave Kelly the same look I'd given her since we were kids, which pretty much said, "Aren't *you* the good daughter?"

After an hour of my teeth clenching, my sister heeded my command and left with Mom. I went straight for the fridge and the wine bottle as soon as they drove off. I didn't think I'd ever understand how Kelly tolerated that woman, and I knew that if I spent as much time with Mom as my siblings did, I'd become an alcoholic.

Dad usually stopped by late in the afternoons, and *not* with my mother. It was nice because we got the opportunity to have some quiet, quality-time conversations that didn't happen often if Mom was in the room because she tended to take over the dialogue. My problem with my food-loving father was that he brought Italian pastries on every visit. I suspected that Dad brought the desserts more for his happy consumption than for mine. That, of course, didn't prevent me from eating them. I also assumed that he ate them at my house because Mom would harass him if he brought them home, and that was something to be avoided at all costs.

Kate, Patty, or Barb came over every day, and each time they brought gifts, from flowers and balloons to chocolates and magazines. Between my friends, Gabby, and my father, I was going to burst out of my splint from all the treats I was consuming. I had already taken to

wearing sweat shorts and loose T-shirts, and I had no idea
when I would be Zumba-ing again to knock off the ex-
cess blubber that was building up! This depressed me
even further, so I ate more and considered hitting the
stores for larger shorts. The icing on the cake was that my
birthday was in two weeks, and I might well be spending
it on the disabled list, which really stank. I loved my
birthday. Last year had been such a blast!

On the Saturday after my accident, Patty came over.
She had decided that my house looked "too chaotic" with
the scattered kitchen chairs, unfolded clothes in the laundry room, drying dishes on the drainboard, and unmade
beds. So she kicked Neil and Vic out for the afternoon,
armed herself with supplies, and set about cleaning and
straightening up. She even donned a crisp white apron.
With her youthful pretty looks, she could bring in a lot of
business for Maids on Wheels or Merry Maids if she did
a commercial for them. I kept waiting for her to put on
little white gloves too. So much for visiting with poor
little me, though. All I saw was a blur of white as she
scooted about. Finally, after two hours of work, she
joined me for a cup of coffee.

"I took the liberty of invading your closet and bringing down some suitable clothes for you to wear. They're
in the guest bedroom. What possessed you to walk
around in those things?" she declared, pointing disdain-
fully at my shabby, stretchy, fleece apparel.

"Oversized with elastic," was my caustic reply. "You
wore sweats when you broke up with Dave!"

"Perhaps. But they were neat and black and fit me
properly. You, on the other hand, look like a bag lady!

Especially with the plastic bag hanging from that walker!" She rose and pulled me up. "Let's get you neatened up a bit, girl. And a little make-up wouldn't hurt either. When was the last time you combed your hair?"

When she was done dressing me, fixing my hair, and applying make-up to my face, even I had to admit that I looked like a new person. She also rearranged the downstairs of my house so that items were easier for me to reach yet still retained an orderly appearance. *And* she returned the kitchen chairs to their rightful places. I even discovered after Patty left that she had not only picked out two weeks' worth of outfits but also ironed and hung them in a reachable location.

When Barb visited, she brought me—or should I say "brought Vic"?—a sexy lingerie outfit that was so tiny, it looked like it was *made* for a "teddy." Yes, *I* was thinner than my friend, but seriously, folks, did I look like a small stuffed animal? I refrained from saying anything, though, and just prayed that it had more than the average two to five percent of spandex in it. I was thinking more along the lines of fifty percent. Since Barb was the largest of the four of us, she had absolutely no judgment when guessing our sizes. We'd given up on reminding her because she'd inevitably forget. To her credit, at least she'd begun leaving the receipts in with the gifts. I knew what I was doing as soon as this splint was off, and it wasn't "dirty dancing" with the hub.

Kate usually stopped by late evenings. Not a good time for either of us! My normally spunky friend was pooped when she arrived, and I was beat from hauling a walker around all day, so we either sat at the kitchen table and gazed blankly at each other or lay on the couch and stared blankly at the television. It didn't matter; I was happy for the company of my dear friend. We had been comforting each other for thirty-eight years, and words weren't always necessary when it came to girlfriends. Some days it was simply about the companionship.

CHAPTER 32—50 MAY END, BUT 39 GOES ON FOREVER

"Happy birthday!" sing-songed my surgeon as he removed the splint. Apparently, I was a fast healer, so after two brutal weeks of confinement, my leg, along with the rest of me, was free at last! The fact that it was on my birthday was both an upper and a downer, but it was a Friday, so I could celebrate over the weekend. Or at least I thought I could, until his next words: "You're going to have to use crutches for the next two weeks. Your ankle is not ready for total weight-bearing just yet."

Oh no, I thought to myself. *Not the dreaded crutches!* I could tell by Vic's expression that he was thinking the exact same thing.

"Well, my fifty-first year is off to a great start," I

said moodily on the way home.

"Stop complaining! You got the splint off early, and he said you're healing well. That's all good stuff, so no pouting!"

"Uh-huh."

"We'll do something fun tomorrow for your birthday, OK? Pick whatever you want to do."

"I want to finish our romantic Central Park walk."

Vic gave me a sideways look. "Uh-huh."

That night, after Vic, Neil, and Oliver sang "Happy Birthday" to me over two candles stuck in a store-bought cupcake, the girls picked me up for a long-overdue trip to Starbucks.

It was exactly what I needed in my birthday-blues state of mind. I hadn't seen the Starbucks crew since my accident, and they were overjoyed at my visit. I was treated like a (handicapped) birthday girl VIP with guests. Kate, Barb, Patty, and I never had to get up to replenish our drinks. Hot, fresh coffees were brought to our table. We received so much attention that it was more like being at an upscale restaurant than the local coffeehouse. For a little while, I was able to temporarily forget my woes and celebrate my special day.

"As soon as you're back on your feet," giggled Kate, "we'll go sing and dance at Crony's. But you have to be in tip-top shape. No one's going to try to pick you up with that impaired look you have going on." (More giggling from the three of them now.) "And honestly, Jill, you scare me with those things. Don't forget, I've seen you in crutch-action before."

Kate was interrupted by a lot of movement as every

Starbucks employee who was working approached us, singing "Happy Birthday"! One of them carried an over-sized slab of chocolate cake adorned with whipped cream, mocha sauce, and candles. The next thing I knew, most of the patrons joined in too. This was a first-time experience for me, and honestly, I thought it was pretty cool. It wasn't every day that a bunch of strangers sang to you. By the expressions on the faces of my girlfriends, I could tell that this was a surprise to them, too, which made it even more special. I felt loved. The cake looked scrumptious. There were four forks in it, so we passed it around, taking turns enjoying a delectable bite.

"And our kids make fun of our Starbucks addiction," said Barb, waving in the direction of our young friends. "But where else could we get the service and attention that we get here?"

"The funny thing is that Neil will make sarcastic re-marks about me coming here, but he never turns down the Frappuccinos or coffees that I bring home for him," I replied. "Come to think of it, he never offers me money for them, either."

"Like that's ever going to happen," laughed Kate. "I'm still buying and paying for gifts from my son to his dad. When does that end?" Her face took on a puzzled expression. "Now that I think about it, I'm still buying and paying for my *own* gifts!"

"Anyway," interrupted Patty as she handed me an envelope, "we have a little something for you for your birthday. It was a last-minute chip-in. Actually, I suppose now it's more of a get-well present."

I took the envelope, saying, "You three have already

done so much for me! This isn't necessary." Inside a very humorous "chick" card was a gift certificate for a day of pampering at a very exclusive spa in the area.

"Wow, girls! This is awesome!" I exclaimed. "And definitely something I could use right now! I retract my previous words. I'll take it! A mani, a pedi, *and* a massage! That's all that I need to feel like a new and happy woman!"

"I took the liberty of booking your day of delights for tomorrow. I'm going with you. I could use a little spoiling too. I've been working so many hours lately," said Kate. "We'll have a nice girls' day out. And I won't take 'no' for an answer."

"Well, I don't have any plans other than dinner with Neil and Vic, so tomorrow's as good a day as any. At least my nails will look good! Maybe I should get my hair done too, if there's time."

"Great! It's all settled, then. I'll pick you up at eight-thirty. Our first appointment is at nine."

We spent another hour making summer plans and catching up on the latest gossip while I silently tried to calculate if I could lose the weight to fit into my new bathing suits or if I should say "the hell with it" and buy new, bigger ones. I didn't relish the idea of another bathing suit shopping debacle, so I vowed to begin a strict salad-only diet on Monday. I'd hang the suits from the cabinets above the fridge and snack areas as my constant diet reminder. Worst-case scenario, I'd spend my days at the beach in shorts and tanks. I'd done it before.

The following morning, Kate arrived on time, and we spent the next five hours being pampered from head to toe. She requested that I bring a nice outfit to change into afterward because she was taking me out for a birthday luncheon. She wouldn't tell me where we were going. She said it was a surprise. I noticed that Kate had been acting nervous all day, more than her usual state. Plus, she kept making what she thought were discreet phone calls. I had a sneaking suspicion that Barb and Patty were going to show up for lunch as another "surprise," which was fine by me. I really didn't get why that would be a secret though.

For my birthday lunch, I chose to wear an olive-green-and-white leaf-print sundress and olive suede thongs embellished with silver peace signs. I donned my favorite pair of silver and marcasite peace earrings, which Neil had given me for Christmas. With the French manicure and freshly styled hair, I didn't look half bad for a fifty-one-year-old. *Yuck!* I had actually thought the number.

By the time we were dressed and ready, it was three o'clock and I was starved. I hadn't consumed anything other than coffee that morning and glasses of lemon water during spa time. Maybe I should start my diet today? Nah. I wanted something big and fattening to eat for lunch. Vic had suggested that we go to dinner tomorrow instead of tonight, so I intended on indulging for lunch now that I didn't have to save my appetite for dinner.

"Kate? I have to ask. What's with you today? You're tapping your fingers on that steering wheel like you're being given a typing test. Shouldn't you be feeling relaxed by now?"

"Yeah. Yeah. I'm sorry. Just lots on my mind lately.

With work, you know?" She gave me a sideways look to see if I was buying the excuse. *Whatever.* I'd go along with her.

"Never mind. Let's go eat. I'm starving!" I pretended to believe her excuse.

"Do you mind if we stop at your house for a minute? I need to print out directions to the restaurant."

"But you have a GPS, Kate."

"I know, but it's not recognizing the address. You know how stupid these things can be!"

"Let me try," I said and reached out toward the screen.

She slapped my hand out of the way. "I said it's not recognizing the name."

Actually, she had said the "address," but I wasn't about to correct her. She seemed to be in a grumpy mood and was fidgeting more than ever. I sat back and listened to the music. It didn't matter if we stopped at my house anyway. I wasn't in any rush.

I sang along to Maroon 5's "Moves Like Jagger," and after a minute Kate joined in. It was an upbeat, infectious song, and by the time we arrived at my house, I was so engrossed in singing and car-seat dancing that I failed to notice the unusually large number of cars on the block.

"I really need to pee! Use the computer in the front room while I go," I said to Kate as we got out of the car.

When I was done in the bathroom, I looked around for Kate, but she was nowhere to be found. It didn't take much to distract my friend, so I headed toward the kitchen, thinking that she was already chewing Vic's ear off. I spotted her outside on the deck with my husband and son.

Yup! She had gotten a hold of both their ears. I laughed. Now I was going to have to drag her out of here, and she hadn't even printed the directions yet!

I stepped out onto the deck, totally focused on the three of them, but a second later, it registered in my head that there were decorations all over. Just as Vic, Neil, and Kate turned to me with huge smiles, it dawned on me that this was my real surprise. My family and friends stepped out from their hiding places on the side of the house, yelled "Happy birthday, Jill!" and broke out into very loud singing of the birthday song. My mouth dropped open before an earsplitting grin took over. Even though I was genuinely smiling, tears formed in my eyes. I was touched, surprised, and somewhat overwhelmed! I wasn't an easy person to trick, and yet they had pulled it off without a hitch. Even with Kate's nervousness and hushed phone calls today, I'd never dreamed that a party was in the works, especially since I had experienced a great one last year.

Kate was the first to envelop me in a hug, followed by Vic and Neil. Everyone else, with Patty and Barb in the lead, talked and laughed as they made their way up the deck stairs to welcome the birthday girl. Right behind my closest friends were the Noodles and Mrs. Funnier. What a great idea to invite them! I hadn't seen them in weeks. Kate thrust a glass of sangria into my hand, and I stood rooted to the spot: greeting, hugging, kissing, and taking sips in between.

Finally, I was able to sit down and take in the "thirty-ninth birthday" decorations, the food, and the guests. I couldn't believe that a year had gone by already. There had been many changes and adjustments in the past twelve months, from Neil's leaving for college to my sitting here with my twenty-fifth-anniversary sprained ankle. Much of it had been good stuff—with the exception of Patty's losing her boyfriend to another man, of course.

I sat there thinking about my fiftieth year and came to a positive conclusion. Despite the fact that I would remain unwilling to admit my age to others, I had actually enjoyed being fifty. Well...fifty-one now. Yeah, there were new wrinkles, weight gain, sagging boobs and butt. And let's not forget the wild and crazy hormonal attacks, hairs sprouting where they shouldn't, people calling you "ma'am," and a son who was fast becoming a man. But there was a positive side too. I had three girlfriends who had stood by my side and one another's for most of our lives, and who would continue to do so, and I could now spend more time enjoying their company. I had a great man to grow old with, and a son to bring me joy for many years to come. I could look forward to grandchildren, whom I would get to spoil without feeling guilty about it, because I was their grandma and that's what I was supposed to do. Now that Neil was in college, Vic and I would be able to spend a lot of much-needed couple time. I felt a deep sense of freedom, as if my life was becoming more about me and my wants and needs, and less about everyone else's. It was all good!

Kate, Patty, and Barb played hostesses as they mingled with the other guests. I could still clearly picture them the first day they approached me outside school and commented on my rust-colored shirt. Who would have thought that we'd still be the best of friends after all these years? I didn't think any of us had changed much. We were just "slightly" older, smarter versions of our twelve-year-old selves. Oh, and definitely better dressed.

My mother and father conversed with Mama Castillo, who actually laughed at something Dad said. She tended to have a soft spot for my father anyway, and the man could probably entertain the Pope with his quick wit and great stories. Whether or not Mama understood what he was saying was a whole other ballgame.

Oh my God! Was I seeing correctly? I blinked, and then blinked again. My advertisement-for-polyester mother was actually dressed in cute denim capris with a pretty, soft, animal-print, *cotton* tank top! What the heck was with that? I happened to catch my sister's eyes, and she nodded toward my mother and smiled. Ah! Now I understood. She must have taken Mom shopping. I gave her the thumbs-up. Maybe our mother was finally moving forward from the sixties with her fashion sense. Then again, only time would tell.

Papa seemed to be taking Ed Noodle on an inspection of my fence. He pointed at it, and Ed nodded. Perhaps he was volunteering to help build one for the other senior. It certainly wouldn't surprise me. They also could be criticizing the fence company that had installed it. Papa, as a former construction worker, never thought other people's work was up to his standards.

Someone turned on a boom box, and Kate attempted to teach Gertrude and Matilda what looked to be some of our Zumba moves. The older women giggled. I suspected they had already indulged in a drink or two. They kept bumping into one another as they wiggled, did some funky arm movements, and kicked their legs up. I wasn't entirely sure which dance it was supposed to be. It looked like a Latin chicken dance. Regardless, they were having fun. Out of the corner of my eye, I spotted Gabby rushing over to join them, her well-endowed chest bouncing with each step. Oliver was putting on his own little dancing dog show, which just amounted to a lot of jumping up and down. Actually, he didn't look much different from the rest of them.

Neil, Jason, and Lou Jr. huddled around Anthony, who appeared to have something small in his hands, since they were all peering down. I'm sure it was another new creation. The boys looked mesmerized, which led me to think it was probably some sort of mini-*Playboy* magazine or something to that effect. I decided to leave them alone for now. At least their ears were bud-free and they were socializing.

Aunt Marie, who was also a Zumba girl, herded Uncle Al, Pete, and Barb's cell-carrying husband, Jerry, over to join the other dancers. I had no doubt that the second she let go of their hands, the three would run for their lives and their dignity. Barb and Patty were right in back of the men, though, so I doubted that they would get very far.

"Are you enjoying yourself? Were you honestly surprised?"

I turned to my husband, threw my arms around him, and planted a long kiss on his smiling lips. "Yes to both questions. This is incredible! Thank you! I love you so much!"

For a while we stood there with our arms around

each other's waists and watched our crazy family and friends. Aunt Marie had taken over the Zumba "class," and everyone had either joined in or was watching the hysterically fun show. Eventually, Kate, Barb, and Patty broke away and joined us on the deck. Kate popped a bottle of champagne, handed us glasses, and poured. Then she gave her camera to Vic.

The four of us gathered closely together in front of a "Happy 39th Birthday" sign and raised our glasses.

"Happy birthday, honey!" said Barb.

"We love you!" added Patty.

"To girlfriends!" toasted Kate.

Cheers!